She heard the piercing screech of tires

Roz turned in time to see a dark sports car come squealing up the driveway toward Crumpet. The bulldog cocked his head at the noise, but was clearly too tired to move quickly. A scream rose in her throat, and her legs began to move as she raced toward the dog. She felt Jamie brush past her, his legs pumping incredibly fast, then she saw him dive for Crumpet.

He caught the bulldog in the chest, and both he and the dog went crashing into the bougainvillea bushes that lined the wide drive. The car slammed into the back of Roz's car, metal grinding against metal with a sickening sound.

A dark-haired man got out of the sports car and began to run back down the driveway. Without thinking, anger bubbling up inside her, Roz began to race after the man.

She was halfway down the drive when the man turned, and she saw the gun in his hand....

ABOUT THE AUTHOR

Like Rosalind, the heroine in *Billion-Dollar Baby*,
Elda Minger has loved animals all her life. One of
her favorites was Charlie, the asthmatic bulldog
she had as a child—and yes, like Crumpet, he
did use sunscreen and watch television.
(Readers may remember Charlie from *Touched
by Love*.) Unable to ignore an abandoned
animal, Elda has placed many strays with
families and stopped counting when the number
passed one hundred. Her most memorable
rescue was during a cross-country trip, when
she picked up a sick dog at a rest stop in
Arkansas and found him a home in Bel Air,
California. Elda makes her own home in
Hollywood, where she lives with three former
stray cats—including Henry from *Bachelor Mother*.

Books by Elda Minger

HARLEQUIN AMERICAN ROMANCE
  12–UNTAMED HEART
  95–ANOTHER CHANCE AT HEAVEN
106–TOUCHED BY LOVE
117–SEIZE THE FIRE
133–BACHELOR MOTHER

Billion-Dollar Baby

ELDA MINGER

Harlequin Books

TORONTO • NEW YORK • LONDON
AMSTERDAM • PARIS • SYDNEY • HAMBURG
STOCKHOLM • ATHENS • TOKYO • MILAN

To Debra Matteucci.
This one was yours from the beginning.
And in memory of Charlie, the real-life Crumpet.

"The love of money is the root of all evil."
—Geoffrey Chaucer

Published August 1986

First printing June 1986

ISBN 0-373-16162-X

Chapter One

I can't stand it anymore.

Rosalind closed her eyes tightly as the limousine swept out of the circular drive. She didn't want to look back and see the Bel Air mansion she'd just left. She didn't want to think about the confrontation she had to have with the cook later in the evening. And she especially didn't want to think about having to hire a new butler.

A gentle, snorting sound pierced through her unhappy thoughts, and her hand automatically reached down to scratch Crumpet's head. She opened her eyes and studied the dog thoughtfully.

Nothing too out of the ordinary there. Just a white English bulldog with a smashed-in little face, a black button nose and a large, slobbery pink tongue that he used often to get her attention. Crumpet, she'd found out very shortly after his care had been entrusted to her, had a disposition that alternated between that of a lion and a lamb—but his appetite was more like a lion's. He wasn't too pleased with her—the first thing she'd done after moving into the Barrett mansion was to put him on a very strict diet.

Well, you are a very fat bulldog, she amended silently. *A grossly spoiled bulldog.* Crumpet snorted as if he could read her thoughts and butted his broad, furry head against her hand, demanding more petting. Oh, he was an ordinary dog in many ways, but there was one rather large difference.

Crumpet had several billion dollars at his disposal.

Rosalind sighed and glanced out the tinted window. Palm trees flashed silently by as they passed one elegant house after another. There was no particular style the area favored—English Tudor sat next to Spanish stucco, and both were across the street from antebellum South.

It was all too much.

And how ironic that a week ago you could barely pay your rent, let alone afford groceries—and now you're on your way to the supermarket in a limousine.

Crumpet snorted again, and she scratched. Closing her eyes, Rosalind willed herself to relax.

Take each day as it comes. Try not to let it get to you. You're really doing quite well—and at least Crumpet is prospering.

Her mind wandered as the limousine continued its smooth progression, and she thought back to how she'd first made Crumpet's acquaintance.

IT HAD BEEN RAINING that evening. She'd stopped up on Hollywood Boulevard to pick up a new mystery at Pickwick's. She'd been rounding the corner, walking slowly to avoid slipping on the sidewalk, when she saw the silver Mercedes.

The car barely stopped as the passenger door flew open. A dark bundle was flung out the door and into the entrance of the small alley behind the bookstore. Tires spinning against the rain-slicked street, the car squealed away.

When Rosalind saw the bundle start to move, she felt the familiar disgust and pain twist her stomach. Another abandoned animal. Perhaps a child. Nothing surprised her anymore, not after her work at the local animal shelter.

Breaking into a run, she reached the sodden bundle within seconds. It was wheezing, and she placed her palms on it, her paperback tucked underneath her arm.

"It's all right. It's all right." She had crooned the words, singsong fashion, until she managed to untie the top of the scratchy burlap bag and push the layers of sodden cloth aside.

A face so ugly it was cute looked up at her, the dark eyes confused. When she tried to pet the small white bulldog, it shrank back, and Rosalind's eyes stung sharply. An abused animal. Again.

"I'm not going to hurt you," she said, watching the dog carefully as she reached into her raincoat pocket for the bag of treats she always kept with her. Feeling around, she grasped one of the doggie crunchies and pulled it out, then held it underneath the bulldog's nose.

"Would you like a little—" The words were barely out of her mouth when the dog grabbed the treat, crunching it noisily.

At least the wheezing stopped. Rosalind helped the dog out of the burlap and ran her fingers gently over his chubby body. When she reached his left hind leg, the dog yelped.

Another vet bill. Just what I need.

Within the hour, she had the dog tended to. A very slight sprain, the vet said, nothing a few day's rest wouldn't mend. Within two hours, the bulldog was warm and fed and sitting in her living room, in front of her television set calmly watching the *Bill Cosby Show.*

Rosalind picked up the battered copy of *TV Guide* and thumbed through it. "There's a Fred Astaire movie on at nine. How does that sound?" She had lived alone for most of her life, and was in the habit of talking to her animals. There was nothing like an old movie—especially with Fred and Ginger—to chase away reality. Movies—the more entertaining the better—had always been her way of escaping when life became too ugly.

The bulldog snorted, then stretched out full-length on the living room floor, his massive head between his paws.

As usual, Rosalind put ads in the local papers and alerted most of the veterinarians in the area. Almost a week went by without any response before Matthew Barrett called.

His voice had rasped over the line, and it seemed to Rosalind that there was so much repressed pain in the old man's tone.

"Is this Rosalind—the young lady who has the white bulldog?"

"Yes, this is she." She glanced down. Crumpet, along with her German shepherd, Sheba, and a Labrador-mix puppy with enormous paws she'd picked up by a freeway entrance, were noisily eating a very large bowl of kibble.

There was a moment of silence; then Rosalind asked softly, "Did you lose your dog?"

"I'm not sure what happened. Crumpet wasn't in his yard when I came home one evening."

Rosalind trusted her instincts—this man didn't seem the sort who would throw helpless animals out of cars. He sounded too concerned.

"I found him in Hollywood. Where do you live?"

"Bel Air," the old man said crisply, in a tone that Rosalind guessed meant he was used to giving orders.

"It's a long way for a dog to travel," she said carefully.

"Unless he had assistance—and I'm sure he did," Matthew replied grimly. "Tell me the truth, now—how did you locate this dog?"

Rosalind related the story quickly. As she did, she glanced at the dogs. They were finished eating, and the puppy was trying to chew on Crumpet's ear. The bulldog snorted but seemed pleased. Rosalind smiled. No matter how depressing it could be to work at the shelter, her animals always cheered her up.

"Hold on for just a second," she said. Then, setting the phone down on the counter and getting down on her knees, she snapped her fingers.

"Crumpet! Come here, Crumpet!"

The bulldog looked up, then tore out of the kitchen, the puppy hot on his heels.

Rosalind stood up and grasped the phone receiver. "I don't think it's your dog," she said. She was beginning to feel sorry for the old man. He sounded as if he missed his bulldog immensely. "When I called his name, he ran into the other room."

She was surprised when Matthew started laughing. "You've got my dog, all right!" He suddenly sounded full of vitality. "Tell me, does he gaze up at you when you try to eat dinner?"

"Yes, but a lot of animals do that."

"But does he lick your ankles and try to get your attention?"

"Yes." She was beginning to smile.

"Does he enjoy the television?"

"Does he ever—especially the dog-food commercials. He goes wild and attacks the screen."

"You've got my Crumpet, then. Could I come over and get him?"

There was a wistful tone in his voice she couldn't refuse. *He sounds as if he's lonely without his dog.* "Of course."

It was only when she hung up the phone that Rosalind realized the state her apartment was in. On the first floor of a Spanish stucco building, it was a cramped one-bedroom affair. The kitchen and living room were really one room divided by a counter. There was barely any closet space, and one small bathroom.

But her landlady, an eccentric Mexican woman, didn't care how many animals she had as long as she kept them clean and quiet. And for Rosalind that had been the major selling point.

As she gazed around her, her spirits sank. Though she had painted the living room white and papered the kitchen with blue-and-white checks, the linoleum still looked old, and the wooden floor was scarred. Her furniture was a jumbled mix of inexpensive pieces she'd bought and hand-me-downs from friends. She hadn't vacuumed today, and dog and cat hair bloomed everywhere.

"Oh, Lord," she said disgustedly as she ran her fingers through her dark auburn hair.

She was exhausted as she heard a car pull up in the driveway, but she forced a smile and opened the door. The man being assisted out of the sleek limousine was fragile and silver-haired, dressed in a very subdued, very expensive gray suit. He looked directly at Rosalind and studied her through the screen door.

"Is it all right if the car is parked here?" he asked.

She nodded her head even as she watched the curtains in the apartment across from her move. Most of her neighbors were older—and nosy. They would probably think the worst as usual, that she was hooking on the side. Or had a sugar daddy.

As Matthew Barrett entered her small apartment, Rosalind forced herself not to think about what he was used to. Bel Air was one of the wealthiest areas in the world. She was sure her home looked like a slum to a man of his tastes.

But all thoughts flew out of her head as Crumpet came tearing into the living room with her two dogs in hot pursuit. The bulldog was running so hard he was wheezing noisily.

"Crumpet?" Matthew called softly.

The dog stopped, then stared. His stumpy little tail began to wag, then his entire rear end. He was wriggling with joy as he threw himself at the old man.

Rosalind found herself with tears in her eyes as she watched the happy reunion. She picked up the puppy so it wouldn't continue to run after the bulldog and nip at his heels and simply let the dog and master reacquaint themselves.

When Matthew finally straightened up from his kneeling position, his eyes were suspiciously bright, and Rosalind was surprised to hear his voice quiver.

"I can't thank you enough."

"It's all right," she answered quickly. "I'm just happy you have him back."

Matthew reached into his suit pocket. "I want to give you a reward—"

"No." At his look of surprise, Rosalind felt she had to explain herself. "I would have done what I did for Crumpet for any animal. I—I work with a shelter, and I've been picking up strays all my life."

He had studied her then, for a long moment, the pale blue eyes sharp and clear, thoughtful. "Then you can't have any objection if I send a check to your shelter. For the animals."

She had been deeply touched. "That would be lovely."

So Crumpet had climbed into the limousine, and Rosalind had stood out on the front stoop and waved as Matthew and his dog went back to their life in Bel Air.

And that is that, she had thought.

Usually when an owner came for his animal, she rarely heard from him again. But Matthew proved to be the exception. Within a week he had called her and asked her to lunch at his house. Rosalind refused at first, but the old man had been persistent.

"Crumpet's been pining for you. I think he misses the company he had at your house."

She'd laughed then and agreed to come.

And so Rosalind found herself falling into a pattern. Every Tuesday afternoon she drove her battered green Toyota into Bel Air and had lunch with Matthew and Crumpet. Matthew was a widower, and Rosalind sensed from the start that even with three grown children, he was a lonely man. She didn't get the feeling he missed his wife all that much; he was simply happy to have someone to talk to. Someone who shared his interests.

And, most important, someone who didn't want anything from him.

Crumpet was the link between them. He adored Rosalind, and she thought she would always remember the frightened, wrinkled face peering out from the folds of burlap. That she and Matthew both loved animals passionately served to forge a very special friendship. During those weekly lunches, their bond tightened, and Rosalind found herself looking forward to Tuesdays.

It was a very special break from the bleakness of her life at home and at the shelter. Rosalind never got used to seeing the worst of human nature during the course of her work, and it never failed to depress her. Not that she didn't have friends or go out to see a movie now and then. But it was so pleasant to sit out by the pool on the flagstone patio and eat lunch off of expensive china and drink champagne out of a crystal goblet.

She could almost believe that life could be beautiful, after all.

There was one afternoon in particular she remembered. She and Matthew had finished lunch and walked out to the gazebo. Matthew had built the small summerhouse last year, and it was a restful place. Mostly white lattice, the gazebo boasted a profusion of hanging flowering plants. It was a cool place to stop and rest. "A little island within the world where one can pause and refresh one's soul," he had said the day it was finished.

He had had something on his mind that day—Roz was sure of that. Crumpet took off at a brisk trot to investigate some bushes, and Matthew patted the cushioned seat next to him.

"Sit with me for a moment, Rosalind." His tone was quiet, reflective.

So she sat, then laughed as her eye caught Crumpet trying to catch a butterfly. The contrast between the clumsy moves the bulldog made and the graceful flutterings of the butterfly amused her, and when she looked back at Matthew, she was smiling.

"I don't have to tell you that I love you very much," he said slowly.

She hadn't felt strange about her friend's declaration. Roz knew exactly what Matthew meant. They had shared so much despite the short time they had known each other.

"I was always grateful to Crumpet for bringing you into my life. I only wish it had been sooner."

She covered his hand with hers, feeling the slightly cooler skin, the veins so close to the surface. She wished she could have given Matthew part of her youth, her strength. More than anyone she had ever met, she wanted to be a help to him, a comfort. There were so many times she had caught a wistful expression on his face, and she knew he regretted growing older.

"I love you, too."

Matthew cleared his throat gruffly, then fixed her with a steady gaze. "I may ask you to do a favor for me someday."

"Anything."

"I know you won't enjoy it. And in the beginning you might not understand it."

"But I would do it for you."

"I know that." He stared out over his estate. Matthew's silences had never unnerved her. They were friends of the sort who were comfortable with silence.

"In time, you'll understand why I ask you."

"Nothing too taxing, I hope." She was joking now. Something about the seriousness of his tone frightened her. She felt as if someone were walking cool fingers up the length of her spine.

"Something that will demand all the courage you have, all of your heart and mind. I know you're not a terribly strong person, Rosalind. You've always been too sensitive. The world is too harsh a place for a girl like you. You're a delicate little thing, and I know all you've ever had is heart. But that's the most important thing. If you're frightened or scared and I'm not around to talk to—"

"Matthew, please."

"If I'm not around, you take the reins and follow your heart. Listen to that voice inside you. There aren't many people in my world who even realize they have that voice, let alone listen to it."

"Matthew..." She *was* scared now. He knew something. But he wasn't going to tell her.

He was making it sound as if he were no longer going to be a part of her world, and that frightened Rosalind. Her earlier years had been lonely and confusing, her mother providing very little stability for her only child. So Rosalind had come to the conclusion that nothing in her world would ever be permanent and decided that kind of thinking couldn't possibly hurt her. She was good at pretending to herself, convincing herself she didn't *need* anything stable or permanent.

Then Matthew Barrett had come into her life.

The mansion he lived in seemed as old as time. It was a solid, imposing structure. Their Tuesday luncheons rolled around like clockwork, and Matthew never missed one. If anything, Rosalind would have to cancel because of an emergency at the shelter. Matthew Barrett represented the first permanent relationship she'd ever had with an older person, and he filled a secret place in her heart that had never known a father's love.

She suspected he knew. He'd drawn her out from the beginning, made her talk about the loneliness and confusion that had filled her childhood. And he had started her back on the road to liking and believing in herself.

"You may have to learn to trust someone besides yourself." He continued talking now, his voice slightly gruff. "But then, you're too much of a loner already, and that would be good for you."

Impossible. "Matthew, I don't think—"

"It will change your life forever, Rosalind. It will change it for the better. Trust me."

"I do."

"Believe in yourself."

"I'll try."

"You'll do just fine. You're just like my Crumpet." He indicated the bulldog, who was rolling wildly in the grass, scratching his back. "All heart, willing to go the distance for someone you love. Bulldogs possess nothing but heart, you know. There was that one I was telling you about that belonged to the butcher..."

And she had relaxed then, knowing the story. In the last few months, Matthew had begun repeating himself, forgetting. She loved him, and other than making sure he saw his doctor regularly and took good care of himself, there wasn't much she could do. There was no one she would rather sit with in the sun and listen to.

It had been one of their last talks.

Almost two years after she met Matthew, she was watching the news and heard of his death. It was Sunday afternoon, and she'd been thinking about the following Tuesday. Rosalind felt completely numb as she watched the newscast, and tears filled her eyes slowly as she realized she had lost a very special friend. Despite their differing ages and financial status, she had felt closer to Matthew than anyone else in her life.

As she'd crawled into bed that night, she lay awake and wondered what would become of Crumpet.

She didn't have to wait long. Matthew's lawyer called her within the week, and she was summoned once again to the house in Bel Air. Crumpet was nowhere in sight, but the dark, paneled library was full of tension. Rosalind sat toward the back. She wasn't worried. Knowing Matthew, she was sure he'd simply left the shelter some money and requested she be there to represent the organization.

So she was totally unprepared for what the lawyer had to say.

"To my children," the lawyer read quietly, "I leave what the law compels me to." He then named off what, to Rosalind, seemed an incredible amount. But as the lawyer continued, she wondered suddenly just who Matthew had left his enormous fortune to.

And then, within a minute's time, the lawyer read the words that changed her life forever.

"And so I leave the bulk of my estate, consisting of houses in Bel Air, Monte Carlo, Paris and Switzerland, and the apartments in New York and London, along with major shares of my company and the balance of my moneys, to my beloved English bulldog, Crumpet." The lawyer cleared his throat and paused amidst complete and total shocked silence. "And as I am of completely sound body and mind, I realize Crumpet cannot possibly oversee all this by himself. I wish to have Miss Rosalind Locklear act as executrix of the estate and take care of Crumpet for as long as he lives."

The room had blurred for an instant, Rosalind had been so shocked by what Matthew had done. The silence in the library was broken, first by one angry voice, then another.

"Damn it, this can't be correct! Father had to be out of his mind!" This from a dark-haired man in his early forties. Matthew Barrett IV—Matt, Rosalind thought silently as she watched the man continue to argue with the lawyer, his aristocratic cheekbones flushed with anger. Two older women joined him, and from their light blond coloring and the expensive way they dressed, Rosalind guessed they were Matthew Barrett's daughters, Sarah and Elizabeth.

She tuned out the argument as the door to the library opened and Tom, the Japanese gardener, walked in, leading a terrified Crumpet by his leash. The bulldog was straining against his lead, panting furiously, his eyes wild. Rosalind started to get out of her chair. But before she could move in the animal's direction, Crumpet saw her and began to bark, jerking his leash. Tom saw Rosalind, and he let the dog go.

He barreled toward her and jumped into her lap, and she felt his nails clawing furiously in the skirt of her blue shirtwaist dress. Her arms went up around the dog, and she held him.

Poor thing, to be in the center of such a mess. It was several seconds before she realized *she* was the center of attention in the quiet library.

"Just what kind of a relationship did you have with my father?" Matt demanded. His color was still high, his tone scornful.

"And why would Daddy leave all his money to that—that hideous beast?" Elizabeth demanded, near tears. "He must have been senile!"

Sarah was right behind her sister, and she put her arm around Elizabeth as she studied Rosalind. "Elizabeth, calm down. You'll make yourself sick."

But her sister was not to be comforted. She continued to glare at Rosalind, her eyes venomous. "Well, I'm sure you think you've won this first round, but I can assure you, Miss Locklear, I'm going to fight this will and break it if it takes forever!"

Rosalind eased Crumpet off her lap and took hold of his leash. Panting and wheezing, the bulldog lay down beside her, gazing up at her with undisguised adoration.

"I certainly don't want any of your money," she began quietly.

"How easy for you to say!" Elizabeth shrilled, but Sarah shushed her.

"Let's hear what Miss Locklear has to say," she suggested.

"Yes, let's hear what the little tart has to say," Elizabeth demanded. "Daddy always had a weakness for women with green eyes!"

Rosalind felt her face flush with color. Her hands started to shake, but she gripped the leash tighter, determined not to break down in front of these horrible people. Matthew had told her all about his family. She had spent one Father's Day with him; they had taken Crumpet and Sheba to a park and walked them for miles. She had never met his children before, had never seen pictures in Matthew's home. The only thing that had ever made them seem real were the postcards in the older man's study. All from expensive cities in Europe and the Orient.

All asking their father to send more money.

He hadn't liked any of his children; she was sure of that. Matthew had been deeply anguished by the way all three had turned out, and he had told her they had been cursed by his money. And by his wife, a woman who had been determined that her children would have the best life could offer.

At any cost.

"I'm not a tart," she said, her voice firm. "I met your father when I found Crumpet wandering about Hollywood. Matthew was convinced someone deliberately dumped him from a car." It was a shot in the dark, but she gave each of them a long, level look. Matthew met her gaze, belligerent. But Elizabeth couldn't quite meet her eyes, and suddenly she *knew*.

Money or no money, Rosalind had never had anything but contempt for people who abandoned a helpless animal.

"Your father loved Crumpet, and from what I observed, the dog gave him a hell of a lot more happiness than the three of you put together."

"How dare you speak to me this way!" Elizabeth exclaimed. She stepped forward, her palm raised.

Before Rosalind could react, Crumpet did. The bulldog shot out, moving astonishingly fast for his weight, and clamped on to Elizabeth's ankle with his jaw, nipping her sharply.

Elizabeth screamed, kicking her expensively shod foot into Crumpet. But the bulldog held on, centuries of breeding and bull baiting manifested in the tenacious hold he maintained.

"My God, Matt, he's attacking me!"

Before Matt could do anything, Rosalind knelt down. "Crumpet, let go."

The bulldog obeyed, quickly trotting behind her, panting and wheezing.

"He ruined my stocking! And there's a mark on my leg!" Elizabeth's face was a mask of mottled fury. "I'm going to have that monster declared rabid and put to sleep!"

"He could have broken your ankle," Rosalind said, raising her voice just enough to be heard above the ruckus Elizabeth was making. "He behaved the way any good dog would."

"By attacking my sister?" Sarah asked sharply.

"She was about to attack me," Rosalind pointed out, determined to give no quarter.

Matt held up his hands, his expression controlled. "Ladies, please. Let's see if we can discuss this like rational adults."

Rosalind was instantly suspicious. In her experience, rational adults were the worst to deal with. At least with children you had a chance, if all their natural emotions hadn't been destroyed.

"No, I don't think so," she said quietly. The astonished surprise in Matt's face, followed by quickly controlled rage at her taking control, told Rosalind she'd made an enemy—and a formidable one. "You can set up an appointment with my lawyer." Her attention was caught by Crumpet's wheezing behind her. "Crumpet is clearly upset by this entire day. I'm going to take him for a walk in the rose garden. I think you all know the way out."

And with that she turned on her heel and walked out of the library.

My lawyer, she thought dazedly as she walked down the long hall toward the back of the mansion. *That's a good one. You've never consulted a lawyer in your life!*

But she kept walking until they were out in the yard, kept walking over acres of lush, green, perfectly maintained grass.

She stopped at the white Victorian gazebo and walked inside. There was a spigot and dog bowl, and after she got Crumpet some water, she splashed a few handfuls over her own face.

"Matthew, why did you do this to me?" she whispered softly. Of all the places she'd been since the older man's death, this was where she felt closest to him. They had often brought picnics here, then walked the dogs and talked of many things.

When she heard noisy slurping, she glanced down. Crumpet practically had his head buried in the water dish. As she watched the dog drink, she knew why Matthew had chosen her.

Crumpet wouldn't have lasted a minute with any of the Barrett children. He would have been thrown out of another car. Consigned to a pound. Or taken to the vet for one last injection.

I could just see Elizabeth, she thought grimly. *"Oh, poor little Crumpet, he can't* live *without my father! It would be cruel to make him go on when he's so unhappy!"*

And so convenient for you.

"Oh, Crumpet," she said. "What are we going to do?"

ROSALIND LEANED FORWARD as the limousine pulled into the parking lot of Ralph's Market in Hollywood.

"Jesse, could you keep the air conditioning running? I don't want Crumpet to get overheated. I'll turn on the TV for him. I should only be a minute, okay?"

"Fine, Roz." Jesse—formerly Jesus, but he hated the name and had changed it—had lived in her building until she'd moved into Crumpet's mansion. A struggling actor, he was lucky if he made it to two auditions a month. She'd asked him to come with her, offering him a job as chauffeur. Tired of working nights at a bar in Marina del Rey, he'd accepted eagerly. She needed someone she knew at the mansion, someone she could trust with Crumpet.

Jesse was a rock.

His dark eyes danced in his tanned face. Roz had often marveled at his bone structure. He was a beautiful man, with thick, wavy dark hair and straight white teeth. He was going to make it, it was just a matter of time.

He'd been a godsend, agreeing to help her out. Their relationship was like that of siblings, friendly and teasing. He had been another stray she'd added to her collection.

She searched through her purse to make sure she had her coupons. It was the only way she'd managed to stay sane on those weekly trips to her old market. Not that she really bought too much, for groceries were delivered to the mansion every couple of days, and the cook did the rest. But she felt so isolated in the huge house. Getting away and walking through her old market helped her keep in touch with her former life. There was nothing like grocery shopping and remembering her past to put everything in perspective.

Reaching over, she snapped on the nine-inch color television and tuned it in to a *Love Boat* rerun. Crumpet barked excitedly as he saw the cruise ship skimming over the ocean.

"You'll be safe, Jesse. I don't think there are any dogs for Crumpet to go after in this one." Laughing, she opened the limousine door and slid out of the sleek car.

TRISTAN JAMES CAMERON, private investigator, glanced impatiently at his watch, then stood up and walked quietly to the window of the Barrett library.

She should have been here by now. What kind of game is this Rosalind playing?

If it had been anyone else, he would have been out the door already. But he couldn't leave. Not this time.

You have to get this job. There was simply no other alternative. He had to infiltrate himself into this household and find out the truth.

He glanced up as one of the maids came into the library with a basket of roses on her arm. She worked quietly and efficiently, putting blooms in the vases on the low satinwood tables around the room. The smell of freshly cut flowers began to permeate the air.

Come on, Rosalind; don't keep me waiting all day.

He had to admit that the circumstances intrigued him. Billions of dollars given to an English bulldog? It sounded like something out of a soap opera. The media had had a field day, and endless articles had been run speculating why Matthew Barrett had left his fortune in the hands of an asthmatic bulldog and a twenty-seven-year-old woman.

It didn't make any sense on one level. *But then all the pieces will fall into place when you meet this Rosalind, won't they?*

The press had been rather unsuccessful thus far. Rosalind Locklear maintained a low profile. The few times she'd strayed out of the house and been pursued by photographers, she'd been quick enough to put her hands in front of her face or avert her head. But he'd see her today and have a chance to make his own assessment of her character.

What he'd found out about her so far had captured his interest. No one knew much about her past, he couldn't even find a record of her high school graduation. All he knew was that she worked at an animal shelter in Hollywood. Her neighbors had told him she had a reputation for taking in strays and finding them homes. At last count, the old woman across the driveway had told him smugly, she had four cats and two dogs.

He glanced at his watch once again. She was almost thirty minutes late for his interview. *For anyone else I'd walk, but for this woman* . . .

His thoughts were interrupted by the sound of the front door swinging open and a symphony of sounds. A dog wheezing, his toenails clacking. And a voice. A clear, soft female voice.

"Jesse, let's get the box in the kitchen. We have to feed them fast if they're going to make it."

The door slammed shut as Jamie got to his feet.

"Come along, Crumpet," the voice said, the slightest bit of sternness present. "Don't dawdle, this is life and death."

Curiouser and curiouser. He got up off the soft leather couch and walked to the entrance of the library.

His first impression was of clouds of dark auburn hair and long legs encased in well-worn jeans. A kelly-green tank top exposed smooth white skin and covered small, nicely shaped breasts. Her feet were bare.

As she came closer, the bulldog at her heels and a dark-haired man walking briskly after her, he noticed the heart-shaped face, upturned nose and a smattering of freckles.

And the deepest green eyes he'd ever seen.

He cleared his throat. "Miss—"

She didn't even break stride. "Oh, my God! Jamie, I forgot all about you! Just follow me, please. I've got an emergency on my hands."

Without questioning her—which he thought later was very strange, because he usually questioned everything—he fell into step behind the dark-haired man carrying the box.

They stopped in the enormous kitchen. Crumpet promptly went over to his water bowl and began to slurp. The box was set on the butcher-block island in the middle of the cooking area, and he watched as Rosalind—for this *had* to be Rosalind—carefully opened it.

"Damn these people," she swore softly.

He watched, amazed, as she lifted out seven little kittens of assorted colors and fur lengths. They were tiny things, their ears still rounded, their eyes barely open.

She glanced up at him. "Watch them for a moment, please?" There was the strangest, most imploring look in her eyes, and he found himself nodding.

"I'll get the eyedroppers, Roz," the dark-haired man said as he bounded out of the kitchen.

Who is this man? Jamie glanced back at the kittens and barely had time to sort out his confused thoughts before he heard a popping sound. She was opening up cans of something, then pulling various ingredients out of kitchen cupboards and mixing the entire mess together.

"I think we can save them if we get something in their stomachs. They don't look like they've been abandoned too long."

Abandoned? He glanced down at the kittens and realized they were way too young to have been separated from their mother.

"I'm really sorry about this, Jamie. I don't normally keep people waiting, but this was an emergency, and the kittens had to come first."

She was a brisk, no-nonsense woman, and he found himself beginning to smile. "I understand. The interview can wait." He reached up and loosened the knot of his tie, then took it off. As he shrugged out of his suit jacket, her voice stopped him.

"If you want to wait in the library, I'll be there within fifteen minutes. Otherwise, we can reschedule—"

"Let me help you," he said quickly. There was no better place to observe someone's personality than in an emergency. This would be the perfect way to see Rosalind's true character.

She smiled then, and her face lit up, transforming it from simply pretty to dangerously close to beautiful. "Thanks." Her tone was soft and heartfelt.

"Hey, don't mention it. I grew up on a farm." *That much at least is the truth.*

The dark-haired man bounded back in, eyedroppers in hand. He handed them to Rosalind, then turned. "I'm Jesse, the chauffeur. You must be—"

"Jamie Cameron. The prospective butler."

They shook hands quickly, and Jamie could tell Jesse was sizing him up. What was this guy's relationship to Rosalind, anyway?

Within a minute, Rosalind placed a bowl with something that looked like cream in it on the table, and each of them had an eyedropper in hand. Jamie watched covertly as Rosalind expertly picked up the smallest kitten and put the dropper to its tiny mouth.

"Come on, baby, drink this, okay?" Her manner was soft and maternal, and Jamie felt a part of his reserve being destroyed. He felt as if he were melting. How could he possibly suspect someone who would rescue a box of abandoned kittens?

Jesse had a kitten in his hand, so Jamie reached for another of the smaller ones and sat down on a chair. With the kitten on his thigh, he stroked the tiny head and guided the filled dropper toward its mouth.

The kitten ate vigorously, then promptly threw up all over his suit pants.

"Oh, no! I'm sorry, Jamie." He looked up to see Rosalind staring down at him, another kitten in her hands.

"It's okay. It'll clean. I just hope I can get some of this stuff down him."

She nodded her head, and he noticed that her green eyes were warmer as they studied him.

The three of them worked silently until all seven of the kittens had eaten. Then Rosalind fixed them a fresh box with a warm piece of material in it and placed the little animals carefully inside.

"In another couple of hours we have to feed them again," she said, addressing her statement to Jesse.

He rolled his eyes. "It's nothing I haven't done before."

"Can you watch them for a while? I'll take Crumpet."

"Sure thing."

"Oh, and the groceries, Jesse. They're still in the limo. I forgot—"

"Take it easy, Roz. I'll get them."

For a moment Jamie envied their casual closeness. Then Jesse left, and he continued to study Rosalind. She snapped her fingers. Crumpet sat up from his prone position on the kitchen floor and trotted over to her feet. He sat down and looked up at her, his large pink tongue lolling out of his mouth.

"We can go into the library and discuss the job, Jamie."

He nodded his head.

"Would you like something to drink before we start? It's hot outside."

"Whatever you're having is fine."

She poured two glasses of apple juice and carried them into the library, Crumpet dogging her every step. Jamie followed, amused by the way the rotund bulldog scrambled to keep up with her brisk pace.

Once they were seated across from each other on the two couches flanking the marble fireplace, Rosalind began the interview.

"I don't know what you've been used to in the other houses you've worked in, Mr. Cameron, but this is a very informal place. *Please* don't call me Miss Locklear or I'll be forced to fire you."

He started to grin.

"The only thing I cannot tolerate is if you're cruel to any of the animals. I was hired to look after Crumpet, and I consider that a tremendous trust Mr. Barrett gave me. So I don't want any of the staff falling short and treating the animals badly. Especially Crumpet. He's been through a very tough time, and I want him to recover."

"You've clearly got a fan in that dog."

She smiled then and ruffled the bulldog's ears. "He's a good boy. It's not his fault he's in the middle of everything."

"I agree."

"And I will not tolerate any gossip leaked out to the press. Matthew's name has already been used to sell too many tabloids. The whole thing has become a circus, and I just want something of a normal life again. Do you understand?"

"Yes." She was standing firm, but he sensed that if he pushed her, she would bend.

"So, do you know what a butler is supposed to do?" she asked.

She seemed a little nervous asking the question, and suddenly Jamie realized she wasn't simply eccentric; she had absolutely no idea how to run the house or what the servants should be doing.

This was going to make things so much easier.

"Of course," he said, deliberately injecting a note of confidence into his voice. *After all, I've watched Sebastian do his job long enough.* He'd also taken a crash course from his personal butler before flying down from San Francisco. Though he had thought he was coming to this particular job completely unprepared, Jamie realized that his scant knowledge, as compared to Rosalind's nonexistent understanding of what a butler actually did, was going to make things easier than he'd thought.

He could see her face visibly relaxing, the wary eyes warming even further. Her face was too open, too expressive. It was the kind of face that could get a woman in trouble if she wasn't careful. His instincts told him that Rosalind had no idea of the stakes involved or how tough she was going to have to be to maneuver her way through the game that was sure to be played.

"Then you're hired." She stood up, and Crumpet stood with her, almost seeming to mimic her motion. "Can you be moved in by tomorrow?"

"This evening, if that's all right with you," he said. There was something about her that touched him. As if she were a child struggling to maintain a semblance of order in a world rapidly going mad.

"That'll be fine." She held out her hand, and he closed his fingers around hers, noticing how delicate her bones were.

Lady, you are completely out of your depth. And you know it.

"I'll see you tonight, then." She turned her gaze to the bulldog. "Okay, Crumpet, time for your run."

Jamie watched and tried not to laugh as the bulldog slowly slid onto the Oriental carpet, a look of disgust on his wrinkled features.

"He doesn't like exercise, I take it."

She looked him directly in the eye. "As much as I cared for Matthew, he wasn't the greatest disciplinarian. Crumpet is much too heavy, and we have to get that weight off him as soon as possible."

They stood staring at each other for a few seconds, Crumpet perfectly still on the carpet and obviously not wanting to be noticed. Then Jamie cleared his throat, breaking the silence.

"I'll see you tonight, then."

"Okay, and thanks for helping out with the kittens."

She walked him to the door, and he felt her watching him as he started down the drive toward his car.

"Jamie?"

He turned around and looked at her, leaning in the doorway, Crumpet by her side.

"I didn't have to interview you."

He remained silent, wanting her to go on.

"The way you didn't get mad when your suit was ruined—I knew right then you were the man for the job."

"Thanks, Rosalind." He tried the name out on his tongue, liking the feel of it.

"Roz, please. Only my mother calls me Rosalind."

He laughed then and started down the drive, hearing the door shut softly. But when he reached his car and slid in behind the wheel, he was no closer to answering any questions than he'd been when he'd been waiting in the library.

Who was Rosalind, really? Why couldn't he find any record of her past life? What had her involvement with Matthew been?

And most important of all, why had Matthew left Crumpet—and Rosalind—his entire fortune?

Chapter Two

Jamie lay back on his bed, hands behind his head, and stared at the ceiling.

None of this makes any sense. Yet.

It was clear Crumpet worshiped Rosalind. The bulldog followed her all around the house, his dark doggy eyes adoring. And Rosalind Locklear was a tough taskmaster. He was amused and quite touched by her determination to make sure Crumpet lost weight and maintained a normal life-style.

He stretched, then settled back on the bed. He'd moved in all of his things five days ago and was beginning to understand the unique household rhythm. Basically, he wasn't a butler, simply a man around the house. Yes, he answered the door and showed various people inside. He stood by Rosalind on the few occasions Matthew's children came to visit—which had been extremely unpleasant. And he supervised some of the other servants.

But he didn't wear a uniform.

"Nice jeans and a shirt are fine with me," Rosalind had informed him the first day.

His life was pleasant. The work load was light, mostly helping Rosalind with various animals. She had turned part of the stables into a modified shelter. Though most of the animals were still at the shelter in Hollywood, she brought some of the "special cases," as she called them, to the mansion.

They were heartbreaking. Mostly pets he was sure no one would ever adopt. Thin, sickly kittens. Frightened, neurotic dogs. There was a nasty parrot, two gerbils that were busily chewing their fur off and a snake that looked as if it were ready to curl up and die.

And she loved them all.

This woman could not possibly have killed Matthew, he thought, studying the pattern of the wallpaper on the far wall.

But had she loved him? Had he loved her? He had known Katherine Barrett had not made her husband happy and he'd also known of Matthew's brief affairs. After all, when a man's marriage essentially ended when he was in his thirties, he couldn't be expected to lie back and die, could he?

But Matthew and Rosalind. It doesn't fit. I just don't think so.

He sighed. Jamie was honest with himself. Ruthlessly. It was what made him so talented in the line of work he had chosen.

It doesn't fit because you don't want it to fit. It would kill you to find out they had been intimate.

He was beginning to really like Rosalind. It was nothing he could put his finger on. Perhaps it was the way she smiled when she got a response out of a particularly damaged animal. He noticed her smiles were reserved for the animals, seldom for people. Except Jesse. He could make her laugh.

And what's their relationship?

He liked the way she walked, a loose-legged gait that was totally unself-conscious. He liked the way she dressed on the mornings he worked with her, in faded jeans and worn cotton T-shirts snug from too many washings. They clung to her slender, shapely body like a second skin.

And she was totally unaware of how good she looked.

Her hair was like a dark red flame, her skin translucent, with just a hint of golden color.

But her eyes...

He'd had dreams about those green eyes. Exactly five nights' worth of dreams. None of them terribly original. All of them variations on a specific theme. He wanted to see her, flushed and satiated, underneath the weight of his naked body. He wanted to see desire, then satisfaction, mirrored in those eyes.

He shifted, physically uncomfortable. *You're a private investigator, not a sex maniac. You have to win her trust, get her to open up to you. And if you keep thinking about her in your bed, you are going to have one hell of a time trying to do your job.*

Her laughter floated up to him then, and he closed his eyes, relaxing and enjoying the moment. He could picture her running on the back lawn with the dogs, getting them to catch the red Frisbee. Crumpet would be tearing clumsily along, but she would encourage him to exercise.

She loves the dog. And she loved Matthew.

He could remember the conversation he'd overheard two nights ago as if it had just happened. The words had burned into his brain. He'd been walking up to his room, but he'd stopped by the library, seeing a light on. Already he knew that Rosalind was a regular visitor there, that she loved to read. He'd heard Crumpet's gentle snoring and had been about to enter the room when he'd heard Jesse's voice float out into the hallway.

"You really loved that old guy, didn't you?"

Jamie had stood perfectly still, knowing one of the pieces of the puzzle he'd come to solve was about to be answered.

"I loved Matthew Barrett very much. There isn't a day goes by that I don't think about him. Oh, Jesse, why did he have to die?"

There had been unmistakable anguish in her voice, and it had touched something in him deeply. He'd thought the same thing when his mother had phoned him and given him the news of Matthew's death.

She didn't kill him. But she did love him.

He closed his eyes and tried to still his restless thoughts.

"COME ON, CRUMPET, quit hogging the set. Everyone else deserves a turn." Rosalind good-naturedly shoved the bulldog away from in front of the TV and changed the channel with the remote control. Images flashed by, including one of a shaggy dog digging into his food dish.

Crumpet went wild, attacking the big screen. Rosalind quickly changed the channel, then recognized an

old western. *Red River*, with John Wayne and Mont-
gomery Clift. A classic.

"All right, we're going to watch this for a while.
Now, Crumpet, settle down and I'll get you a snack."

At the mention of the word "snack," the bulldog
froze. There was just the slightest movement of his
stubby little tail.

"So you understand the English language," Rosalind teased as she got up off the bed and walked toward the chest of drawers in one corner. She'd stashed
a large box of Snausages there the other evening.

As she looked back at the enormous king-size bed,
she couldn't repress a grin.

Five pairs of canine eyes were locked on her. Especially Crumpet's. Rosalind had moved in her pets,
certain that Crumpet would appreciate company after losing Matthew. So now Crumpet had four dog
friends and one disgruntled cat.

Sheba, her German shepherd, lay sprawled on the
carpeted floor, preferring that to the bed. Her black-
and-tan muzzle was raised, her eyes beseeching Roz
for a treat. Kai, a silver Siberian husky, poked her
head out from underneath the bed, where she liked to
hide. Sting was sprawled out on top of the bed. She'd
never been able to fully discipline the fun-loving lab
mix. He was an enormous black dog with a smooth
coat and two white paws. And Champ, a wiry, cream-
colored bulldog mix, trotted over to her feet and
clumsily sat up on his hind legs. Champ had broken
her heart when she'd found him, his ribs sticking out
and his light coat covered with mud and fleas. He'd
been snarling by some trash cans. Roz had worked
with him for months, tried to find him a home. But by

the time she had gentled him, she had fallen in love with the mutt with the smashed-in face.

Curled up on the pillows by the enormous teak headboard was a ball of cream-colored fluff. Eldin, her cat, was the only feline Rosalind had ever known who could take on such a group of dogs and win. He simply didn't put up with nonsense from anyone. When Crumpet had first met the cat, he had tried to chase him. But Eldin had simply puffed up to three times his size, and Crumpet had turned tail and fled.

Quite a crew, she thought as she dug into the drawer.

"Okay, guys." She held up the box of Snausages and walked toward the bed.

Various commands were softly spoken as she put the animals through their paces.

"Good boy, Champ."

"Catch, Sheba."

"Now, Sting, you only get one!"

"Speak, Kai!"

"Come on, Crumpet. Sit. No, not down. Sit. Sit. Like this." Gently, she pushed the bulldog's hind end down, then rewarded him with his treat.

"Good boy!"

Eldin looked bored with the entire proceedings.

"I'll get you some tuna when I go to the kitchen," Rosalind promised as she secured the box of treats back in the drawer. She hated eating in the immense, cold and very formal dining room, so she took her meals late at night in the kitchen.

It had been a hard adjustment, sleeping in the large, strange house. So Rosalind had taken to walking the halls quietly at night. She thought a lot, mostly about the strange turn her life had taken. And she wished with all her heart she were back at her apartment, immersed in the life she had always known.

Because then Matthew would still be alive.

She blinked her eyes rapidly. The pain was still too fresh, too new. There were times when she expected the front chimes to sound, to see Crumpet go shooting down the long, pink marble hall and come skidding to a stop at Matthew's feet as he opened the door.

It was so hard to believe he was gone forever.

Oh, Matthew, I do miss you. She knelt down and petted Crumpet's head gently, trying very hard not to cry.

AN HOUR LATER she was in the kitchen, an interested Crumpet at her feet. He was relentless, carefully watching for any scraps that might be flung his way. But Rosalind was adamant, she wanted him to lose at least ten pounds. For a bulldog his size, that was equivalent to eighty in a human being.

"So nothing for you, you little mooch," she said, rummaging through the cupboards and taking out a copper omelet pan. Within minutes she had assembled eggs, Swiss cheese, leftover ham and a fresh tomato. After making herself a cup of Swiss mocha coffee from instant, she set about grating the cheese, dicing the ham and chopping up the tomato.

This was the only real time she felt comfortable in the mansion. The cook was in bed, as was the maid. Tom, the man who tended the grounds, was asleep in one of the guest houses out back. She would have welcomed Jesse's company, but she knew he had a commercial audition tomorrow.

And Jamie? What about his company? She had thought about him at odd moments while she walked the halls at night. He seemed nice enough. She had been impressed with him from the beginning, the way he had pitched in and helped with the kittens. But there was something else. She liked the way his blue eyes were so warm. There were slight lines around his eyes and mouth that indicated he was a man who laughed easily, enjoyed life. And he tried to make her laugh. He could tease without making it malicious. She watched him covertly when they worked together, liking the way the sunlight brought out the reddish highlights in his brown hair. She found herself attracted to the way he walked, the grace of his movements.

Roz felt safe and protected by his presence in the mansion. There was something about him that caused a certain warmth to fill her body, a lightness and happiness. He listened to her, never broke into her conversation or gazed blankly past her, not really there. When he was with her, it was almost as if she felt she were a different person, prettier and funnier, less introverted.

He made it so much easier for her to enjoy her time at the Barrett mansion, instead of feeling trapped.

Her thoughts were broken by the slight nudge on her leg. Glancing down, she saw Crumpet gazing up at her, his attention rapt as he studied the food spread out over the tiled counter.

Forcing her thoughts away from Jamie, she remembered Jesse's audition and began to talk to the bulldog. The kitchen was suddenly too quiet.

"I think he's a cornflake in this one," she told an uninterested Crumpet. The dog's eyes were fixed on the chunk of ham.

"You never give up, do you?" She cut off a small piece of ham and tossed it to him. His huge jaws opened, and the ham disappeared.

"That's to give you incentive, Crumpet." She put a small pat of butter in the pan and turned on the burner. "You have to stick to your diet; otherwise, you won't live very long. It's the same for humans, you know."

She stopped talking, suddenly aware. She'd walked the halls enough to know what noises were normal. And this one wasn't. Just the slightest creaking.

But all houses creak at night, don't they? she thought desperately, not wanting to believe there was a stranger inside. Yet the hair was standing up on the back of her neck, and Crumpet growled softly.

She turned off the burner, the omelet forgotten.

"Is anyone there?" Her voice sounded small as it floated out into the darkness beyond the kitchen. For just an instant Rosalind wished she were back in her old apartment, where she could see everything at a quick glance. But Matthew's mansion was enormous, set on five acres of prime Bel Air real estate. It was completely isolated, but the set of elaborate alarms and the panic button in the master bedroom connected directly to the local police department were excellent protection.

Someone is in the house.

Jamie had left almost a half hour ago for a midnight run. If he'd just let himself in, he wouldn't be sneaking around. Jesse was asleep, his bedroom in another wing, as were the dogs. Sheba had been an excellent guard dog, but she was getting old and had trouble hearing. Champ was afraid of men, Sting liked everyone, and she'd put Kai in the kennel out back because she liked to sleep outside. If only the husky were with her now, she wouldn't be as afraid.

Crumpet trotted to the edge of the kitchen linoleum, his toenails clicking. In a part of her mind, Rosalind realized she had forgotten to trim them.

"Stay," she whispered softly.

Crumpet continued to trot slowly down the hall.

Damn it, Matthew, you were a soft touch with that bulldog. But she couldn't let Crumpet walk into a harmful situation. Picking up a rolling pin, she followed the dog.

They were almost to the front door when she heard a noise. Kneeling down and grabbing Crumpet's collar, she dropped the rolling pin, put two fingers into her mouth and gave an ear-shattering whistle.

Within a minute, the other three dogs came thundering down the stairs, barking and yapping, ready to go outside and play. But Rosalind was counting on whoever it was being so scared that he would leave.

She was gratified to hear the sound of one of the screens being ripped out and a dull crash as someone landed in the thick bushes beneath the library window.

"Come!" She called to all the dogs as she raced to the front door, flinging it open and running outside. A shadowy figure was running down the sloping lawn, and Rosalind dug her heels into the lush grass and began to give chase. The dogs followed her, yapping excitedly. To them, this was a wonderful game, because

Rosalind didn't usually go dashing across the front lawn at nearly one in the morning.

The racing figure in front of her disappeared around a bend in the driveway. Bushes lined the drive, concealing the invader. Rosalind sucked more air into her already aching lungs—this was no measured jog; this was all or nothing. She was hell-bent on at least catching a glimpse of the intruder.

She reached the main street, the street lamps giving off a faint glow in the dark, cool night. Pausing for breath, she glanced from side to side, gasping softly. Sting and Sheba jumped up, their paws playfully punching her chest. They wanted to play.

"Damn it." She swore softly, annoyed that she had lost whoever it was. He couldn't have run that far, he had to be hiding.

She began to jog down the street but gave up as she realized she was leaving the house open and completely unprotected. What if the intruder decided to double back and rob the mansion?

She turned then, the dogs at her heels, and ran quickly back toward the house. As she was running up the dark, shadowy drive, she didn't watch where she was going and felt herself colliding with someone.

Fighting the urge to scream, she jerked back, only to realize to her dismay that she was being held closely in a pair of strong, masculine hands.

But the dogs weren't growling.

"Jamie?" she whispered.

"Roz, what are you doing out here?" He was dressed in a pair of sweat shorts and sneakers, nothing else. She could feel the warmth from his body, the clean scent. She stepped back slightly and looked up at him. As her eyes grew accustomed to the dark, she could make out the tautly defined muscles in his chest, the sprinkling of hair. Heat seemed to emanate from his body, and for just an instant Rosalind longed to ask him to simply hold her, to help her believe that someday things would be all right.

Instead, she stepped back. He loosened his hold on her immediately.

"There was someone—someone in the house. They broke in, and I called the dogs and—"

"Someone broke in tonight? Where?" His voice was sharp, all business. Rosalind suddenly sagged against him again, relieved to have someone to share it all with.

"The library. When I called the dogs, whoever it was broke out through the big window, the screen, so I think they came in a different way."

"Come on; let's go back up." With the dogs trotting at their heels, the two of them began to walk back up the long drive. Rosalind was surprised to find that Jamie kept his arm around her. She was even more surprised to find she liked the warmth and security he offered. She needed a friend, someone she could lean on just a little. It seemed she'd been on her own forever, always taking charge of situations. It was pure luxury to share that responsibility with someone so capable.

They walked back into the house, straight into the library. Jamie quickly took in the destroyed screen and dented bushes.

"Whoever it was was big—look at the hole here." He motioned Rosalind over to the window, and she saw the huge expanse of flattened bushes.

"And it had to be someone who had knowledge of the alarm system; otherwise, they never would have gotten inside."

Rosalind walked over to the black leather couch and sat down, her legs shaking. "Just the thought of someone in here—" She stopped talking suddenly as her eye caught something on the parquet floor.

"Oh, my God."

"Roz?"

"Jamie, where's Crumpet?"

"Right here with me."

Her voice was tight. "There's some ground chicken on the floor, right here. Chicken is Crumpet's favorite food."

"You think—"

"We have to get him to the vet."

As if on cue, Crumpet began to shake. The bulldog's sturdy legs gave way, and he fell to the floor and began to convulse.

"I'll get the car." Jamie was out the door in a flash. Rosalind grabbed an afghan she'd brought down the other night when she'd been cold reading and wrapped it around Crumpet, then lifted him up. She barely staggered under the bulldog's weight, adrenaline rushing through her bloodstream and making her head feel as if it were going to explode right off her body.

Out of the corner of her eye she saw Jamie rush in through the front door and run to her side. He took Crumpet out of her arms, and both of them raced to his car.

JAMIE'S FEELINGS were running rampant as he studied Rosalind. The two of them were sitting in the waiting room. She was very still, her face covered by both hands.

He was sure she was crying.

"Hey." He moved closer to her on the couch. "He's going to be fine. You caught it in time. Come on, Roz."

Her shoulders shook—just the tiniest quiver. Doing what he had wanted to do all along, Jamie put his arms around her and drew her against his bare chest.

"It's okay, Roz, just let it all out."

She sobbed then, curling herself into a ball against him and shaking with the intensity of her emotions. And he simply held her, touched her hair lightly, whispered soothing words.

"I failed him, Jamie," she whispered hoarsely, then hiccuped and began to sob again.

"No, you didn't. Crumpet is going to be fine."

"Matthew. I failed Matthew."

He continued to hold her. A part of him hated to get information out of her this way, but it wasn't as if he were asking questions.

"He trusted me, and I just can't do it. I don't understand people like this, people who would poison a dog just so they could—"

She broke off as the vet entered the room, Crumpet trotting behind him on a lead. When the bulldog saw Rosalind, he walked slowly over to her and lay down, resting his head against her foot. Rosalind began to sob again as she reached down and petted the top of the bulldog's head.

Jamie gave her shoulder a brief squeeze, then got up and walked over to the desk and took care of the bill.

"Any special care?" he asked the vet.

"No." Dr. Ramsey was an older man, bald, with fringes of white hair around his ears. "You caught it in time. Crumpet's fine. I gave him something to induce vomiting, and it's completely out of his system. From what Roz said, I'd say it was rat poison. Just make sure she gets some sleep," he said, his glance indicating Rosalind. "She's a strong one, but Matthew put her in quite a predicament."

"You know Rosalind?"

He smiled. "She's brought me more strays than I can remember. That's how she met Mr. Barrett. She found Crumpet wandering around Hollywood. I tell you, that man worshiped the ground she walked on."

The pieces were beginning to fall into place for Jamie. "Thank you. I appreciate your seeing us on such short notice."

"It's my job. I wouldn't want anything to happen to that bulldog." Behind his glasses, his sharp blue eyes twinkled. "It tickled me, what Barrett did, leaving it all to her and the dog. If you ask me, none of those children of his were worth a damn."

Jamie nodded. "I couldn't have put it better myself," he said quietly, his eyes on Rosalind.

"You her husband?"

"No, the butler."

The older man gave Jamie a long, level stare that made it quite clear he didn't believe a word of it. "You take care of that girl. No funny business; you know what I mean?"

Jamie couldn't repress a smile. "I promise you, sir, I'll carry out my duties to the best of my ability."

Dr. Ramsey snorted. "Just do your job."

Jamie drove them home, Rosalind crying the entire way. *This is more than tonight,* he thought. *This is everything that has happened to her since Matthew died.* But he didn't pursue the subject, simply let her cry. Crumpet sat in her lap and halfway through the ride fell asleep, his head cradled in her arms.

"It was the stupid diet," she said as they walked into the house, Crumpet trotting slowly behind them.

"Crumpet's?"

Her voice trembled. "If he hadn't been hungry, he wouldn't have eaten the poison."

"I seriously doubt it. That dog is a canine garbage disposal."

"My dogs are trained not to eat anything except what I give them, but Crumpet didn't know—" She started to cry again, and Jamie fought down the urge to take her in his arms and comfort her.

You can't. You simply cannot get involved, no matter how much you think she's innocent. Not right now.

"What were you doing up?" he asked, changing the subject.

"I was—I was making an omelet."

"I have an idea." *You can't take her in your arms, but you can make life easier for her.* "Go upstairs and I'll make you an omelet and bring it up to you."

"No, I can't have you—"

"Scoot. I'll clean up the library and be up within twenty minutes. Take Crumpet."

He cleaned up the poisoned chicken, checked the window again to make sure it was secure, then went to the kitchen. Finding Rosalind's ingredients all ready and waiting, Jamie expertly made an enormous omelet, then poured a large glass of orange juice, put everything on a tray and headed upstairs.

The sight that met his eyes as he entered the large master bedroom made him smile. Rosalind was sprawled out, asleep, in the middle of the bed, four dogs and a cat surrounding her. She was still dressed in the jeans and T-shirt she'd put on that morning. Her three dogs were asleep, but Crumpet was perched on the edge of the mattress, watching a musical comedy. Men in black tuxedos and women in filmy chiffon dresses were dancing their way down an enormous cake. And Crumpet couldn't take his eyes off the screen.

"Roz?" he called softly.

No response.

He sat down on the edge of the bed, tray in hand. Within seconds, he felt a gentle nudge at his arm and looked over to see pleading brown eyes staring out of a wrinkled face.

"Split it?" he asked.

Crumpet simply snorted.

"You can't tell Roz."

The bulldog's face split into a doggy grin, and he whined.

After they ate, Jamie gently took off Rosalind's sneakers. Her feet seemed so fragile, the bones so delicate. He hesitated for a moment, then unsnapped her jeans and tugged them off. Pulling back the covers, he tucked her in, smoothing the satin comforter carefully over her exhausted body.

Then he lay down next to her, outside the covers.

In case that maniac comes back.

Who are you kidding? You just want to stay close to her.

She needs to sleep. I'll make sure she isn't disturbed.

Tell me another one.

He lay watching her sleep until the movie was over. Crumpet watched the station sign-off, but Jamie drew the line at staring at snow. Picking up the remote control, he clicked the television off, then lay back next to Rosalind and closed his eyes.

Chapter Three

"Come on, boy! You can do it!" Rosalind called encouragement to Crumpet as he paddled furiously in the pool. Water splashed every which way as the bulldog thrashed his fat paws, dog-paddling furiously. She stayed almost two feet ahead of him, making him come to her through the water.

"Just a little bit more and we can stop for lunch."

Crumpet continued to churn the chlorinated water, and Roz watched the dog carefully. There was such a fine line when you exercised an overweight animal. And Crumpet was very fat. Dr. Ramsey had filled her in on how the bulldog had been overindulged by Matthew. At one point in his life, Crumpet had weighed so much he had sat down on his leg and broken it.

Rosalind was determined to see Crumpet live a happy, healthy, *normal* life.

She couldn't run him around too much except in the evenings when it was cool. Bulldogs were notoriously susceptible to heat exhaustion. And she couldn't run him too much, anyway, as fat as he was. It was then that Roz hit on the perfect solution—swimming. She fashioned a clumsy pair of water wings for the heavy bulldog—as top-heavy as all bulldogs are, Crumpet would sink like a stone if he didn't have some support in the water—and managed to make him believe it was all one big game.

So far it was working.

Crumpet began to snort as he breathed, and Roz took it as a signal that exercise was over for the day. Closing the distance between them, she put her arms around Crumpet's barrellike body and began to glide him through the water toward the shallow end and the steps. The bulldog was so fat—and so well supported—that he floated easily.

"You were wonderful today, Crumpet. You're beginning to swim like a fish, you know that?" She set Crumpet gently down on the steps and took off his water wings. Crumpet licked her arm the entire time she was unfastening them, then eased himself up out of the water and collapsed on the cement surrounding the pool.

"Come on, Crump, it wasn't *that* bad."

In answer, the bulldog rolled his eyes, then wrinkled up the skin on his back so it was bunched up around his neck.

"Sarcasm doesn't become you."

"Is that how a bulldog displays sarcasm?" The masculine voice sounded amused.

Roz whirled around, caught off guard. She talked to her animals constantly but was usually alone with them. For some reason, she didn't want Jamie to think she was stupid.

"I—I've seen Crumpet do this before." She stared at Jamie, waiting for the condescending remark, the statement that she was certainly reading more into the animal than was possible. That dogs were dumb animals and couldn't possibly have the capacity to be sarcastic.

"I had a pony when I was a boy. I swear he seemed like he was laughing when he would pitch one of us in a mudhole."

She smiled, feeling herself relax. During the last few weeks Jamie had lived at the mansion, he had never shown anything but kindness and respect toward her. She was slowly beginning to trust him. To like him.

"I was just about to fix myself some lunch," Jamie continued. "There's some salami and cheese in the fridge. I could make us sandwiches, and we could eat out by the pool."

She was touched by his thoughtfulness, and for a moment she couldn't answer. His duties as butler certainly didn't include fixing her lunch. She had told both Jesse and Jamie that they could fix themselves something to eat whenever they wanted to. The cook had been furious and had given two weeks' notice. Roz had been glad to see her go.

"I'd love it. Just let me dry Crump—"

The bulldog moved with astonishing speed for his weight and now sat on one of Jamie's feet, staring up at him adoringly and soaking the leg of his jeans.

"What the—"

"Crumpet has a limited vocabulary, but he does know a few words. Salami is one of them."

"Should I make him something?"

"Nope. He gets Fit and Trim. I measure it out three times a day. Sometimes, for variety, I'll wet it down with a little vegetable broth."

Crumpet snorted loudly, then flattened himself out on the cement, his massive head resting on Jamie's foot.

Jamie laughed, then reached down and scratched Crumpet behind his ears. "I have to admit, boy, it doesn't sound that appetizing." As he scratched the bulldog, he looked up at Roz and smiled.

She caught her breath. There was something in his smile so completely and utterly gentle. It made her want to believe they could become friends.

"Those sandwiches sound super. I'll dry Crumpet off, and we can eat in about ten minutes."

Later, after their sandwiches had been consumed and Crumpet was staring forlornly at his half-eaten bowl of low-fat kibble, Roz stretched out her legs and stared up at the sky.

"It's so quiet here," she said softly. "Sometimes I can't get to sleep at night."

"What do you do?" Jamie picked up the crust of his sandwich and eyed it, then set it back down on his plate.

"I wouldn't do that if I were you. Someone's watching." Roz could see Crumpet trying to sneak toward Jamie's legs. The bulldog's attempts were comical. It was impossible for a dog that size to go unnoticed.

"I won't give him anything. I agree with you that he's too heavy. It's good of you, Roz, to try and reduce him."

"I always argued with Matthew." She glanced away from Jamie, feeling the familiar sting in her eyes. It was still too soon to have consigned Matthew to her memories.

"What do you do when you can't sleep?" Jamie asked.

She smiled at him, grateful he had decided to change the subject. "I walk the halls. Or I go down to the library and find something to read. Matthew has an incredible library. You're welcome to use it anytime you want."

"Have you always liked to read?"

"Except when it's something assigned. Or good for me." She squinted her eyes against the sun.

"You're stubborn."

"Guess so." She could feel herself tightening, the calm she had been enjoying moments before evaporating.

"I didn't mean that in a bad way. Maybe I chose the wrong word. Determined. That's better."

She relaxed again, seeing his smile. "My mother always used to tell me that's how I was. When I wanted something, there was nothing that would stand in my way."

"And you've always liked animals."

She laughed. "To my mother's complete despair. She wanted a clean house, and I brought in regular portions of hair, feathers and mud." She hesitated for a second, then decided to try to explain. Maybe he would understand. "I could never leave them, Jamie. Not one. Even if I saw something moving in the bushes, I'd park the car and get out and investigate."

The expression in his eyes was calm and reassuring, as if he knew she was sharing something special with him. "My mom's the same way. She once stole a neighbor's poodle because they used to leave him tied out on their back porch for hours. All the poor thing did was bark and chew on its rope.''

"She stole it?'' Roz leaned forward, resting her elbows on the glass-topped table. "Good for her. I'd love to have seen that."

Jamie laughed. "Mom could be pretty formidable. The night she stole the poodle, that was all she talked about over dinner. The thing that really fired her up was that they hadn't left any water for the dog. Or else it was so unhappy it had tipped it over. Anyway, all of us kids went to bed, and the next morning the poodle was hiding in our upstairs bathroom."

Roz felt Crumpet nudge her thigh, and she reached down and began to scratch his head. "How did she reconcile that with teaching you all not to be dishonest?"

She glimpsed something uneasy in his expression for just a second as he stared out over the pool. The water reflected the brightness of the sun.

"She just said that sometimes the rules didn't apply. Sometimes you just had to do what you felt was right."

"She's right."

They were silent for a while, and Roz was surprised, because it was comfortable. One of the things she liked the best about Jamie was that he didn't seem to feel the need to talk all the time, to fill the silence. She leaned her head back and closed her eyes, letting the sun warm her face.

She was almost completely relaxed when Jamie said softly, "I think we have company."

The tone of his voice, slightly protective, told her who it was before she opened her eyes and saw Sarah and her son coming toward them. Matthew's oldest daughter was chic as usual, her pale golden hair pulled into a severe chignon, her beige linen suit unwrinkled. Roz was sure that it was a designer suit and that her shoes were handmade and Italian, her blouse silk. Mark, her eight-year-old son, trailed behind her. He was dressed in well-cut pants and a jacket, and Roz wished he had worn a pair of jeans and a T-shirt. Something about the child unnerved her—perhaps the way he followed his mother around like an obedient show dog. She couldn't remember when she had ever seen the child not trailing behind his mother.

"Hello, Sarah."

Roz stood up slowly, every muscle in her body reluctant. Their last meeting had not been pleasant. Matthew's children were contesting the will, but from what the lawyer had told her, Matthew had expected this, and the document was as tight as possible and not open to interpretation.

"Rosalind."

Sarah was the least objectionable of Matthew's three children. She was the most reasonable, the one who inevitably stepped in when Elizabeth became hysterical and Matt demanding. Rosalind didn't particularly like the woman, but she knew enough not to make her an enemy.

"Could we—" Here Sarah glanced quickly at Jamie and with a delicate tilt of her head gave Roz the impression she found his presence less than delightful. "Could we talk privately?"

"Certainly." Feeling at a disadvantage in her white bikini, Roz pushed in her chair and began to walk around the pool to another table. Crumpet got up and began to follow her.

"Mom, look how fat he is!" Mark said.

Rosalind bit her lip and willed herself to walk calmly toward the table and chairs on the far side. What could anyone expect of someone growing up with Matthew's three children as examples?

Once seated, Rosalind said calmly, "Would you like anything to drink? It's been very hot the last couple of days."

Sarah nodded, and Roz noticed that Maria, the maid, was already headed toward them. She had given the girl the job because she had needed it, because she was kind to the animals and primarily because she was Jesse's sister.

"Hi, Maria. Sarah would like—" She glanced at the woman, her eyebrows slightly raised. It gave Rosalind a perverse feeling of pleasure to call Matthew's children by their first names. She knew it irked all of them, but she had no intention of kowtowing to them. Now or ever.

"Perrier with lime. Mark, would you like something?"

The boy seemed uncertain, and Roz decided to try one more time.

"I've got some great root beer."

Mark glanced toward his mother, and Roz saw the question in the child's eyes. He would do nothing until his mother approved.

The sign she gave was for Roz's ears; she was sure of that. "I suppose so." Mark gave Roz a small, nervous smile that flickered off his face so quickly she thought she could have easily imagined it.

"I'll have a root beer, too. Could you check and see if Jamie wants anything?" As Roz said his name, she glanced at him. He was watching them, leaning back in his chair. Though his stance seemed relaxed, she suddenly felt he was anything but.

He's worried about me. The idea came to her gently, so obvious she wondered why she had never thought of it before. There had been only one person in her life who had worried about her before, and the idea of Jamie filling Matthew's place in her emotional life frightened her. She felt a quick flash of anger tense her stomach and wanted to tell Jamie she didn't need his or anyone else's protection, when she again remembered Matthew. He'd always encouraged her not to judge everyone by her mother's actions. Growing up, she had never had anyone she could depend on. Most people couldn't possibly be like her mother. Matthew hadn't been. She didn't think Jamie was. He always stayed close when there was any trouble in the air.

And there was trouble now.

Sarah chatted about several inconsequential things until Maria returned with their drinks. Roz glanced over and was perversely pleased when she saw that Jamie had a can of root beer in his hand.

But Roz watched as Sarah took a sip of her drink, then set it down and leaned forward, her gaze fixed steadily on her.

Here it comes.

"I suppose I ought to commend you. My *father*—" and here Roz noticed she gave the slightest possessive emphasis to the word "—left you with several very generous charge accounts. My brother tells me you haven't taken advantage of any of them."

Rosalind waited, silent. She had learned early in the game that it completely unnerved the Barretts if she didn't argue or even answer at first. Surely Sarah hadn't driven all the way down from her home in Coldwater Canyon to talk about some charge accounts.

"Just for general expenses and food. What else would I want to buy?" Roz leaned back in her chair and tried to look as if she didn't have a single care. She hoped she was succeeding.

"What else, indeed?" Sarah had a way of slightly looking down her nose that made a person feel as if he had just crawled out from under a rock. Roz knew that look and steeled herself against it.

She decided to help Sarah get to the point.

"I know you didn't come here to comment on my spending habits. Your time is very valuable, and so is mine. Why did you want to speak to me?"

Roz thought she saw a flicker of surprise in Sarah's cool expression; then the woman studied her nails casually. Roz glanced toward Jamie. He had finished his root beer; the can had been set on the table. But he was leaning forward in his seat, his hands clasped between his knees, watching.

"As we told you before, my sister, my brother and I are going to contest this will. I cannot seriously believe my father left all his money to that—that wrinkled monster!"

At Sarah's reference to Crumpet, Roz glanced over at the bulldog. He was standing by the pool, and she was surprised to see Mark reaching a tentative hand toward him. Crumpet made a soft sniffing sound, and Roz smiled as she watched the boy's small hand pet the large head. Crumpet's pink tongue flashed out, and Mark laughed as the dog licked him.

"Mark! Mark, don't let that *animal* touch you! He might give you a disease if he licks you. You know what the doctor said!"

"Mother—"

"Mark, *right now*! Remember what we talked about!"

Looking miserable, Mark dropped his hand. Crumpet, sensing his confusion, stood still, merely looking at the boy.

"He has a very sweet temperament," Roz began. "I know bulldogs look fierce, but they're really quite gentle."

"You can't expect me to listen to the virtues that ugly thing possesses! My father left all his money to a *dog*! I will not accept that!"

"A dog that gave him a great deal of pleasure," Roz replied.

"You must have done the same, to be living in the house that should have gone to us." Sarah's eyes were narrowed, calculating.

Rosalind sighed. "Every Tuesday. But not the way you think I did. Matthew had me over for lunch. We talked. He was a lonely man, Sarah, and from what I saw here in two years, none of you did anything to alleviate his loneliness. No one was with him all the time but Crumpet."

"And how convenient for you, Rosalind, to be living here and enjoying all the things my father worked for! You have a setup that will last you the rest of your life! I'm sorry, but I can't accept this!"

"It's not the rest of my life, Sarah. You know that. You know the conditions of the will." Matthew had made his will airtight, and Rosalind now realized he had anticipated his children contesting the document. When Crumpet died—hopefully a natural death—the money would be distributed among several animal agencies across the country. The remainder of Matthew's fortune would be used to start up a halfway house for stray animals in L.A.

"But until Crumpet dies, you have quite a little setup here, Rosalind. Can you see my point? Can you understand that I think this is wrong?"

Knowing it was impossible to explain to Sarah that she would have never willingly chosen this life for herself, Rosalind was about to open her mouth and tell Sarah she thought the conversation was over when she heard a tremendous splash.

When she glanced quickly at the pool, Mark was standing at the edge, looking into the rippling water.

Crumpet!

"He fell in..." Mark began in a wobbly voice. Rosalind barely stood before she saw Jamie bound out of his chair and make a running dive. Water surged up and sprayed over their table and chair. She felt it, cool and refreshing against her bare skin, at the same time she heard Sarah scream. Then, her heart in her mouth, she watched as both man and dog came to the surface of the water. Crumpet looked like a seal, his ears plastered back against his head. His eyes bugged out, and he blew water into Jamie's face through his nostrils.

Supporting the dog's body with one arm, Jamie swam quickly to the shallow end and helped Crumpet up the stairs and into a fresh towel.

Rosalind ran toward them, her heart in her mouth. Crumpet was starting to shake.

"Take him into the downstairs bathroom and turn on the heater. I'll call the vet." As Jamie picked Crumpet up in his arms and headed toward the house, Roz turned toward Sarah. She was furious, her linen suit a sodden mess. Mark's hand was firmly clasped in hers, and the child was looking down at the wet cement.

"I'm sorry, Sarah, but we can't continue this conversation right now. I'm sure you know the way out. And next time, please call before you come over."

"I'll send you the bill for this suit. It's ruined! I'll never be able to wear it again, it'll smell like chlorine!"

"Fine. Now I'd like you to leave."

Once she was sure Sarah and Mark were out of the house, Roz rushed upstairs to the bathroom. Crumpet was dry, sitting on the floor of the immense bathroom with Jamie. The bulldog wheezed gently, and Roz sat down and put her arm around the dog.

"I called Dr. Ramsey. He's on his way."

"Jamie, I wouldn't be that scared except that Crumpet gets asthma attacks when he's under stress."

"He threw up a lot of water. I think he's going to be fine."

"He never goes near the deep end of the pool. He's never fallen in before—"

"Mark pushed him."

"*Pushed* him? You mean that little monster—"

"It was the most halfhearted push I've ever seen. I don't think he meant it."

Crumpet wheezed wearily and collapsed into Roz's lap.

"Whether he meant it or not, Crumpet still fell into the pool."

"He'll be okay. He was only in for a few seconds."

Dr. Ramsey confirmed Jamie's opinion, and when the veterinarian left, Roz leaned back against the door and sighed, closing her eyes. When she opened them, Jamie was still standing next to her in the pink marble hallway.

"I'm sorry I got so upset. It's just that I hate to see bad things happen to Crumpet." She took a deep breath. "Since Matthew died, the dog has never been able to have a normal life. I can't even take him outside during the day and walk him because of the damn reporters. I'm just—I don't know, paranoid."

"You're just a good mother hen. To all your chicks." She was surprised when she felt him put his arm around her shoulders and start toward the stairs. "Look, why don't you go upstairs and sit with Crumpet while he watches some television. I'll feed the rest of the animals. You look pretty beat."

His blue eyes were warm, the pressure of his fingers on her shoulder firm. Again, Roz wanted to lean into him, and for a moment she wondered if he would carry her up the stairs the way he had carried Crumpet into the house. She had been deeply embarrassed the morning after the poisoning when she'd realized he had undressed her and tucked her into bed. But it had been such a tender thing to do, and secretly she had been touched.

Jamie had stood by her today. He had saved Crumpet. Rosalind wasn't sure she could have gotten the heavy bulldog out of deep water by herself. He did far more than any butler was supposed to, and he was a genuinely good guy. She wanted to do something nice for him.

"I've got an even better idea. While you feed the animals, I'll phone for a pizza. There's beer in the fridge, and Crumpet can pick a movie. He's crazy about them, so we have all the cable channels."

"You're on. Anything but anchovies."

"How about one of those with everything on it?"

"Perfect!"

THE EVENING WAS A SUCCESS. Two movies, a large pizza and several bottles of beer later, Rosalind glanced lazily at the clock and smothered a yawn. Two-thirty in the morning. It had been so special, sitting and talking to Jamie. They had laughed through a screwball comedy, then watched Fred Astaire and Ginger Rogers dance their way through another movie. Through it all, Crumpet had stared at the screen, enraptured.

"He really likes all the dancing," Roz said as she rummaged through the carton for another slice of pizza. "I read an article once that said cats like cartoons and music videos because of all the movement. But I've never seen a dog that likes television like Crumpet."

"Did Matthew like television?"

Rosalind started to laugh. After three beers, her defenses were down, and she was feeling warm and relaxed. "He didn't watch a lot." She began to giggle, and Crumpet watched the slice of pizza in her hand tremble. A piece of sausage fell on the carpet, and he darted toward it. "Matthew watched intellectual television. You know, *Masterpiece Theatre*, The Raj Quartet, stuff like that. Crumpet used to sleep at his feet." She stretched her jean-clad legs out in front of her and wriggled her feet. "*I* corrupted him."

"How did you do that?" Jamie was lying on his side, looking up at her.

"When I found him in Hollywood and brought him home, he began to watch the stuff we all watched. Reruns. *Gilligan's Island. The Munsters. Leave It to Beaver.* He even liked the talk shows, especially David Letterman."

"So he was totally corrupted by the time Matthew rescued him," Jamie clarified.

She nodded. "The works. He even likes the soaps. But his favorites are all the Busby Berkeley musicals, and anything with Fred and Ginger."

"That's amazing. How can you tell?"

Roz started to laugh. "If he doesn't like something, he falls asleep. But if he likes it, he'll sit right in front of the screen, perfectly still. It used to make Matthew laugh all the time."

"You said you lived in Hollywood. Is that where you found Crumpet?"

"That's where I saw him get thrown out of a car. Behind Pickwick's on the Boulevard."

She watched as Jamie sat up, his facial expression intent. She was used to this side of him; he was endlessly curious about people in general and asked so many questions. Before tonight, she had been evasive at times. She had never wanted many people to know that much about her, especially her past. But now, with Jamie, she felt some of her inhibitions leaving as he continued his line of questioning.

"So even back before Matthew died, you think his children were trying to get rid of the dog."

"Isn't that sick? I mean, Crumpet made Matthew so happy. I can't understand people like that."

"What part of Hollywood did you live in?"

"On Las Palmas. Right below Fountain."

"I know where that is. In an apartment?"

"Yes. It was mostly old people, and pretty run-down. But the landlady didn't care how many animals I had, and that was all that mattered to me."

"Where did you work?"

"At a shelter on Santa Monica. I still work there; I just took my vacation when I moved here. I wanted some time to get used to the change."

"Do you like it?"

"Here? Sometimes it's okay, like swimming in the pool early in the morning and running the dogs in the backyard. But most of the time it's like living in a fishbowl. Matthew used to tell me he was never really sure who his friends were and had never been sure since he started making all his money. When I was a lot younger, I used to think having a lot of money would be super. Now I'm not sure. Sometimes it can be like a curse, you know?"

Jamie nodded his head.

"I look at his children, and I never get a sense that any of them *loved* him. Sometimes, when the weather wasn't good, Matthew and I would have lunch in the dining room and then go to the library. One time I looked at his desk and there were three postcards. One from Matt, one from Sarah and one from Elizabeth. They were all from Europe. All asking for more money. Like their father was a machine or something.''

"I know what you mean. They all seem obsessed with the money. And so angry it was left to Crumpet."

"He's only a *dog*, not some sort of monster. The way she talked about him today..." Roz stifled another yawn with the palm of her hand.

"I should let you get some sleep."

"No. No, don't go." She was surprised at herself for wanting Jamie to stay. Usually she was content to remain alone. It had always been her nature to avoid large groups of people, to remain apart from the crowd. But living in the mansion was a lonely business, and Roz had enjoyed tonight. It was good to talk sometimes, to let all the emotions boiling inside come to the surface in words and then evaporate.

There was a moment of silence; then Jamie spoke. "Sarah was pretty nasty today. I feel sorry for Mark; that kid always looks so unhappy."

"I wish I could get him alone for about ten minutes. I'd give him a pair of jeans and a T-shirt and take him to a baseball game or something. It isn't right, Jamie, to dress up a kid that age like a little—like a little robot! And he's scared of her; I can tell." She lay back on the floor, her eyes focusing on the ceiling. "It must be a terrible thing to be afraid of your own mother."

"If Sarah were my mother, I'd be scared." Jamie stretched, then stood up as Roz got slowly to her feet.

"I'm sorry; I didn't mean to keep you up," she said quickly.

"You aren't. I enjoyed this evening, too."

She looked away and could feel his eyes on her, studying her. She was aware of the times Jamie simply watched her, and it was unnerving.

"Why do I get the feeling you consider me some kind of rare species?"

He was silent for a moment, and a peculiar tension seemed to fill the bedroom. But Roz wasn't afraid. She knew Jamie wasn't the kind of man to press his advantage. He had done too many kind things for her. And for Crumpet.

"I'm sorry. I didn't know I was being so obvious."

"Do you think I'm some sort of freak or something?" Now Roz knew she was being defensive, but it was as if her emotions had grabbed her and were refusing to let go. It was nerve-racking, living in the Barrett mansion and knowing your every move was scrutinized. That the press usually waited outside, eager to catch a glimpse of you. Or of Crumpet.

At first she had made the fatal mistake of believing she could reason with reporters. The second day she had been in residence at the mansion, she had leashed up Crumpet and Sheba and walked out the front door and down the circular drive to the sidewalk. Within a minute, she had been surrounded by five reporters.

"Rosalind, what was your first thought when you learned Matthew Barrett appointed you executrix of his will?"

"How old is the dog? How long do you think he'll live?"

"Did you and Matthew have a romantic involvement? How did you meet him?"

"Why would Barrett leave his fortune to a dog?"

"Come on, honey, give me something I can use!"

"Smile for me, Rosalind."

She had been terrified as they'd closed in, the flashes from their cameras blinding her. Sheba had barked furiously, and Crumpet had wound his leash around her legs. She had shielded her face with her hands, then fallen on the sidewalk as one of the reporters reached out to grab Crumpet and she leaned forward to prevent the woman from touching him. Scrambling out of the binding leather leash, she had looped her fingers through each dog's collar and darted through a gap in the high hedge surrounding the Barrett property.

Since that day, she hadn't been outside except on the private grounds in back of the mansion, in a car or during her trips to the market.

But the publicity continued. Though the tabloids had slacked off, Crumpet made the cover of *People* magazine. The press now referred to him as the "Billion-Dollar Baby." The article had made Roz cringe, but whoever had written it had loved every melodramatic moment. Matthew had come out looking like the king of an incredible dynasty; his children, like Lear's daughters. There had been a photo of Roz, in jeans and a sweatshirt, walking Crumpet a few blocks from the mansion. That was before she had learned her world had shrunk to encompass only the Barrett mansion and grounds. And even there she wasn't free of scrutiny. Sometimes she caught the servants eyeing her curiously. She knew they were worried about their jobs, wondering what she was going to do, despite the fact that she had assured them all that their positions were secure.

And now Jamie. Why did she get the feeling he wanted something more from her than his job as a butler?

She decided to take the bull by the horns.

"Are you sure that's the only reason you're here?" she asked bluntly.

"What do you mean?"

"I mean, you never struck me as the butler type."

There was something in his face as she made that remark. Something in his eyes, so fleeting. Roz waited, surprised at the slight pain in her chest. She was holding her breath.

"I'm not sure if that's a compliment or not," Jamie replied slowly. "Roz, I'm never going to hurt you. You have to believe that."

Though the beer had made her brain slightly fuzzy, she was still aware of his precise choice of words. *Hurt* her? She had never thought Jamie was going to hurt her. Working with animals, she had to rely on her instincts. And she knew this man was not the destructive sort.

"I never believed that," she said softly. For just an instant, she wanted to reach out and touch his arm, and the impulse frightened her. She had made sure she'd never needed anyone before. Why would she feel this way toward Jamie? It didn't make sense.

He continued to choose his words carefully. "I'm here to do the best job I can. To help you. If you feel I'm not working out—"

"No, it's not that! It's just this feeling I get sometimes. Like I'm an insect in one of those glass display cases and you're trying to determine where I came from." She took a deep breath, all the hurt and anger she'd been stifling rising to the surface. Her voice was low and intense as she looked him directly in the eye. "Jamie, whatever you've heard, I was never Matthew's mistress. When I first talked with him on the phone, I didn't know how much money he had. It was never something I cared about. He was just a lonely old man living in this horrible place." She covered her mouth with her hands, horrified. Her eyes were filling with hot tears, and her shoulders were beginning to shake. She had never, *never*, by a look or word or glance, revealed what she felt inside to anyone. She had kept her feelings private, trying to respect Matthew and his wishes. To keep a little part of herself separate.

She had tried to prevent the ugliness of his world from touching her.

Roz felt his arm coming around her shoulder and jerked back at the touch.

"Don't you feel sorry for me!" She said the words fiercely but felt his arm settle around her shoulder firmly. It was a warm touch, a reassuring touch.

"I don't. Roz, I just want you to know . . . I'm here for you. For whatever you need. It's had to be tough, living here, going through such a—" He wrinkled his forehead, searching for the word. "Such a total invasion of privacy. I never wanted to contribute to that. If you catch me looking at you—I've just always been a person who studies other people."

She was silent, her face averted.

"I don't think you're strange or weird or amusing. I think of you as a—a friend. Could we be friends, Roz?"

The expression in his voice was her undoing. He sounded so sincere, so *caring*. If he was a liar, then he was a damn good one. And suddenly it didn't matter. She was tired of being alone, tired of always shouldering the entire burden. For as long as she could remember, she had been in charge. First with her mother. Now, through no fault of her own, with Crumpet. What would it be like to lean your head on someone else's shoulder and share part of your worries?

The temptation was overwhelming. Perhaps because of the beer, perhaps because of the evening they had just shared, perhaps because Jamie had already helped her through two emergencies. Whatever the reason, she was beginning to trust him. She wanted to trust him. It had to be the most wonderful thing in the world, to be close to another person.

To be able to depend on someone else.

"I think so. I *do* like you, Jamie. I like the way you were with the kittens that first day. The way you are with Crumpet." *The way you are with me.* "I feel as if I can depend on you in an emergency."

"You can depend on me anytime. I want you to know that, Roz."

"Thank you."

She felt his arm slide around her waist; then he was helping her to her feet. "I think we both need to get to bed."

Coming from some other man, the remark might have been suggestive. Coming from Jamie, it was comforting. As Roz stood up, she yawned again. "The beer made me sleepy."

"Me, too."

They stood silently, side by side, the room dark except for the flickering images from the big-screen television. Actors were dancing down an enormous stairway, and bubbles were floating everywhere.

"Crumpet has the right idea," Jamie said as he pulled back the covers on the king-size bed. "I think everyone needs a little fantasy when the going gets rough."

Roz was surprised when he tucked her in gently. He knelt beside the bed, and for one instant she was afraid he was going to kiss her.

But he didn't. Instead, he smoothed back the hair from her forehead with the gentlest of gestures. "Sleep tight, Roz. We'll work it out. Nothing looks as bad after a good night's rest."

And then he was gone.

She closed her eyes, her mind a whirl of jumbled images. Tonight, simple as it was, had been wonderful. To her, feeling close to someone always took such monumental effort. How had Jamie slipped by most of her defenses so easily? How had she lowered her emotional guard long enough to actually believe he might care for her? As a friend, of course.

The credits were rolling. She knew, because Crumpet was whining, curled up into a tight little ball in front of the screen.

"Crump! Get up here! You can come up, boy." Seconds after she spoke, she felt the mattress depress; then Crumpet was licking her cheek, then trotting to the foot of the bed and laying his face at her feet.

Everyone needs a little fantasy. All her life, in her deepest dreams, Roz had thought of being able to look up into another person's eyes and feel close to them. In the romantic movies she watched, it all seemed so effortless. As a child, she had loved the fantasy world she had created for herself. On nights when her mother was out late, she'd never felt alone with the television on. She'd sat glued to the set, absorbing the glamorous clothes, the elegant homes, the witty dialogue. People came together and became friends and lovers so easily. And everything was so beautiful. In her heart of hearts, Rosalind had wished she could step into the small, flickering screen and become a part of that world.

Reality, for her, had been so different. She had had trouble making friends as a child because she and her mother had moved around so much. Later, in junior high, it had been easier to pretend she didn't care. When she'd finally dropped out of school, taking care of animals had filled that emotional void.

She sighed, not wanting to remember earlier years, and turned over on her stomach, flipping her pillow over and pressing her face against the cool surface. Her hand reached down, and she patted the mattress. Within seconds, she felt Crumpet's tongue licking her fingers.

"All I ever wanted was one friend," she said sleepily, finding comfort in the fact that the bulldog couldn't possibly understand what she was saying.

She thought of the look on Jamie's face as he'd smoothed her hair back. The expression in his blue eyes had been so gentle. Closing her eyes, she drifted off to sleep.

Chapter Four

She's more than information, and you know it. Within the space of a few weeks, Jamie's world had been completely turned around. It had all seemed so easy at first. Go to the Barrett mansion. Pretend to be a butler and interview for the job. Get the job. Once inside the mansion, collect all the information you can. Figure out Rosalind Locklear.

Figure out whether she could have murdered Matthew Barrett.

Impossible. The woman he had gotten to know could not have murdered anyone. His impressions were so mixed up. At first he had been attracted to her. Sexually attracted. A simple, biological urge. She was a beautiful woman, whether she realized it or not. Then he had watched her, tried to figure out why a man like Matthew Barrett would leave her in charge of his entire estate. Because Rosalind Locklear *was* in charge. Unless Crumpet suddenly learned to pay bills and balance a checkbook.

What he had seen had impressed the hell out of him. If he had to pick one word to characterize her, it would be *kind*. The way she was with the animals, the servants, Jesse, Jesse's sister, Maria. She was kind to him. He had never worked an easier job. It was simply so comfortable working for Roz. She was there right beside you. There was nothing she asked you to do she wasn't willing to do herself.

But now he was beginning to care for her.

His first impression had been correct. She was way over her head, and she knew it. Her nerves were stretched so tightly at times. But all it took to relax her was a stroll out back, a run with the dogs, a visit to the stable-turned-shelter. He enjoyed being with her at these times. Rosalind, relaxed, was terrific company. He could understand why Matthew had had her over every week.

I would have had her over every day.

She trusted him completely now. He knew, because she left Crumpet with him. The bulldog was walking quietly beside him as he strolled the grounds of the mansion. The rigorous diet and exercise program were beginning to pay off. Crumpet was losing weight; his muscles were beginning to shape up. The bulldog was happier and raced around with the other dogs, hardly wheezing. "He's a regular dog now," Roz had told Jamie quietly one evening. "He's just one of the guys."

And at that moment he had gotten the distinct feeling *she* had never been one of the guys—but wanted it for Crumpet. And the bulldog *was* happier; there was no doubting that.

Jamie could see the roof of the mansion through the trees and picked up speed. "Come on, boy; let's get our blood moving." He began to jog, and Crumpet barked, then nipped playfully at his jean-clad legs as they both ran.

He was in sight of the mansion when he noticed the strange woman sitting out by the pool, a drink in hand. A slender woman in a cream-colored suit, she had strawberry-blond hair pulled back from her face into a sleek bun. As Jamie approached her, he studied her. She reminded him of someone.

Roz. She had the same expression around her eyes, the same full mouth. Their figures were similar. But there was something about her that was different.

"Excuse me; do you know where Rosalind is?"

Jamie stopped at her table and stood looking down at the woman, Crumpet at his side. The bulldog cocked his head, his attention focused on the stranger.

"She's out. She got a call from the shelter. Can I help you with anything?"

"I'd just like to see Rosalind as soon as possible."

"You're her sister?" Jamie asked the most logical question. This woman was definitely related to Roz.

The change in her face was rapid and breathtaking. She smiled, then tilted her head prettily. Jamie was sure she knew exactly how she looked, what effect she wanted. No, this woman wasn't like Roz. Except on the surface.

"You are the most *darling* man. Didn't Rosalind tell you I was going to be visiting? I'm her mother."

"Her mother? You can't—" He stopped, amazed he had voiced his thoughts. Normally he had better control.

"Aren't you sweet! No, I'm her mother, and I can't understand why she isn't here. It isn't like Rosalind to be so irresponsible."

"She'd be here if she hadn't received that call." For some reason he felt compelled to defend her.

"Is she still working with those animals?"

"She still works at the shelter."

The woman sighed. "I suppose I can't complain. I mean, look what happened." Then she noticed Crumpet, and her eyes lit up. "So this is the billion-dollar baby!" She frowned. "Is he eating enough? He looks like he's lost weight."

"He's been on a diet. He's doing fine, Mrs.—"

"Deena. Just call me Deena."

"Deena."

They chatted for another twenty minutes; then Jamie saw Crumpet perk up his ears and whine. Roz was home.

"Let me get you another drink," he offered. Deena didn't refuse, so he took her glass and walked quickly in the direction of the mansion.

Inside, he heard Roz, her voice floating down the hall as she talked with Jesse.

"There's a kennel empty down in the stable. She'll have to be inside, though. I don't want to take the chance of—"

"Roz, your mother is here. She's out back." As Jamie walked up to the two of them, he noticed Jesse was carrying a large box. And Roz's face was tear-stained, her eyes red.

"Damn." The word expressed so much frustration, all held in reserve. Her green eyes were strained, and there was a tightness around her mouth. "Jesse, would you go out and talk to her a little? Stall her? Jamie, could you carry this up to my room?'' She indicated the large box in Jesse's arms.

Within seconds, the box had switched hands, and Jamie was looking down at the most pathetic creature he had ever seen. It looked like an Irish setter. Barely. Its ribs were showing clearly through a dull, matted coat. Around its neck, the fur had been rubbed off and the skin chafed until it was bloody. The dog was so still it might have been dead, except for the slightest, almost imperceptible movement as it breathed. And it smelled, mud and waste clinging to its fur.

He swallowed. He'd studied the animal for mere seconds and couldn't understand how Roz could still hope.

''Let's go,'' she said quietly.

He followed her up the stairs into her private bathroom. She motioned for him to set the box down on the tiled floor.

''Dr. Ramsey should be here shortly. The dog won't eat anything; he'll have to give her a vitamin shot. But's she's going to live.''

''How can you be so sure?'' Jamie couldn't take his eyes away from the dog in the box. Even Crumpet was subdued, and Jamie could feel the bulldog pressing his body against his legs.

''If she fought this long, she isn't going to give up now.''

''Where did you find her?''

''In an alley, next to a dumpster. Some kids were poking at her with sticks. An old woman called the shelter, and we went down to investigate.''

Dr. Ramsey was there within minutes. He checked over the animal, and when he talked with Rosalind, his eyes were grave.

"This animal is going to need a lot of time and attention."

Roz nodded.

"She won't be fit as a pet for anyone. You know that."

"I'll keep her, then."

"She's running a slight fever. I gave her an antibiotic and some vitamins. Let her sleep, and once she wakes up, see if you can get something down her. Baby food, rice, something bland. I'll be by tomorrow." He rubbed his hand wearily over his forehead. "Rosalind, it would be easier if we just put her down."

"Is she in pain?" The question was so soft, Jamie barely heard it.

"She's not in agony. But I don't know what she'll be good for. There are welts underneath the fur. She's been beaten. Starved pretty badly. It's a long haul with this one, a major commitment. If you want me to put her down, I'd understand."

Jamie could see her eyes filling with tears. It seemed strange to him that it was not easier for her by now. She'd told him she'd worked at the shelter for years. How many animals like this had she seen?

"I'll take my chances."

"Call me if you have any questions."

After the doctor left, Roz knelt down by the box. She moved slowly, gently, as she reached out and put her hand on the animal's head. "There you are; you're safe now. No one is going to hurt you now. There's nothing to be afraid of. I'm going to leave you for a little bit, but then I'm going to bring you some food as soon as you wake up, and you're going to eat it and get better." Jamie watched as her hand faltered the slightest bit. "You're going to get better; I know you are."

He watched her as she sat next to the box, slowly stroking the dog's head. There was no sound in the bathroom other than the setter's labored breathing.

When she finally turned around, he recognized the expression on her face. She had pulled deep into herself again and shut herself off. At first he had mistaken it for shyness. Then he thought she was slightly cold. Later he realized it was the way she dealt with pain, separating herself from emotion.

"Jamie, I'm going to go down to talk with my mother. Could you stay with her for a while? If she wakes up, try to get her to take some water. I shouldn't be longer than half an hour. I just have to find out what she wants."

As he watched her leave, he realized how tired she was. Her words would have never been as revealing. "What she wants." What kind of a mother was Deena if the first thing her daughter thought of when she saw her was what *she* wanted? A few weeks ago, Jamie would have been delighted at the arrival of Roz's mother. The woman would have been a perfect source of information; she would have helped him find out so much more about Roz. But now all he could think of was helping her. Being a friend.

The dog's breathing brought him out of his thoughts, and he moved to the side of the box and sat down, stretching his legs out in front of him. His hand went to the bruised head without any hesitation, and he began to stroke the fine fur, the feathery ears.

"It's okay, girl. You don't know it, but you've stumbled into the arms of the best mother in the entire world. If anyone can help you get better, Roz can." He continued to stroke the dog's head, his voice soft and reassuring. "But you have to do your part, you know. No one's going to hurt you here. Nothing else is going to happen; no one's going to poke you with sticks. You're going to be fine." He studied the dog's face, wondering how on earth anyone could abuse an animal this way. It made him sick. As a child, he had been deeply affected by his mother's work, and even though the family had laughed about her midnight poodle rescue, it had moved him.

"So you just hang in until Roz gets back, and then you'll know you're in the best hands. She won't let you die. I've seen her at work. I think she's on to something. If you believe hard enough—"

He stopped talking as the dog's face flickered. Then, with the slightest movement, one eye opened slowly, and Jamie looked at the most purely frightened expression he had ever seen. He felt his eyes sting but continued to slowly stroke the dog's head. Within less than a minute, the eye closed, the dog took a deep breath, and the skin underneath his fingers quivered slightly.

"That's a good girl." Jamie continued to touch the dog, but he stopped talking as his mind drifted. The expression in the animal's eye—it had reminded him of something. What? His fingers continued to skim over the matted fur, the welts around the dog's shoulders and back. Where had he seen that expression before?

The simple movement of his hand brought the image back sharply. He had been stroking Rosalind's hair the night he had tucked her in. Though the light had been dim, he hadn't mistaken that look. She had been frightened of him. Not in a sexual way. Simply frightened. As if a part of her had given up and expected bad things to happen.

His throat felt tight. Jamie swallowed, then looked back down at the dog and continued to pet it. His thoughts were taking him by surprise. More than anything, he wanted to replace that fearful look with a smile. He had seen Roz smile, but only with her animals. The day the kittens she had rescued all found homes, she had laughed and talked over dinner, describing each family. She had been exuberant, excited. She had reminded him of his mother, the way she looked when she had taken on the world and won.

He rarely saw that expression directed at another person.

"HELLO, MOTHER."

"Hello, Rosalind. How are you?"

"Fine."

There was an awkward silence; then Rosalind said quietly, "What was it you wanted to see me about?"

"I need your help, darling. I'm getting married."

"Again?"

"Now don't you start! This time I know he's the right one. I met Harold at a barbecue in Dallas. You remember Susannah Barlow, the woman who married that oil man? Well, she gave this party, and the minute I saw Harold . . ."

Rosalind tuned out her mother's excited voice and reached down to scratch Crumpet's ears. A long time ago, almost fifteen years ago, Roz had decided never to care again. Her mother was incapable of that sort of decision. Each time, each man, each marriage, was going to save her, make her life complete. Deena had rushed headlong into six marriages. Harold would be number seven.

For as long as she could remember, Roz had wanted a father. Each man had tried to fill the role, but most of them hadn't known what to do with a little red-haired kid. Some had brought her candy. Others had taken her places—to the circus once. But none of them had ever talked to her. Deena rarely had the time, either. It had taken Roz years of introspection before she realized that basically Deena had been the child and she had been the parent. Pregnant at sixteen and a mother a year later, Deena had thought of her as a doll. But dolls weren't as inconvenient as daughters were. Deena had wanted someone who would love her forever, with no reservations. Someone who would never leave her.

Roz had left at fifteen.

Deena's third husband had given her a kitten. Roz had been seven at the time. A fat, gentle man, Ted had taught her about responsibility. He had told her she was responsible for her pet, for making sure it had food and water. Roz had taken the kitten to bed with her, and when the rough little tongue had licked her face, she had fallen in love.

From that time on, no animal was too ugly, too old, too much trouble. She had loved them all, and to Deena's despair, taken them all in. School had seemed a waste of time, now that she knew what she wanted to do. She'd started working in the shelter in eighth grade, then quit school in the ninth. No one had questioned her as to why she could work any hours given her. And no one had come after her as she'd feared. When they moved to Hollywood, Deena forgot to register her in school.

Roz never mentioned her past to anyone. And she refused to feel sorry for herself. A voracious reader, she considered herself as educated as the next person. And in a strange way, once she was out from under her mother's roof and no longer "Deena's daughter," she gained perspective. She accepted her mother the way she was and realized this was all she was capable of giving. In her own way, Deena loved her.

Matthew Barrett had been the closest she had ever gotten to a real father. Over the two years she had seen him, he had managed to find out the entire story. They had talked for hours, and Roz credited Matthew with starting her on the road to liking herself again. He had made her understand why so many of her bad feelings were connected to her past.

She had argued with him at first. "People always leave, Matthew. Nothing is permanent, and the sooner anyone accepts that, the happier they are."

"Love is permanent." He had looked at her fiercely that day, his eyes stern underneath the white brows.

"Maybe for some people."

"Maybe for you."

"I don't think so."

"What makes you think you're so special? Why should you be different from anyone else?"

"I just don't have time for that stuff."

"You *must* make time for essential things, Rosalind."

"Matthew, let's talk about something else. Please."

But he had been persistent, as dogged as Crumpet was when he chased butterflies. And in the end he had exacted a promise from her.

"Don't turn your back on love when it comes your way, Roz."

"But how do you know?"

"When a person's happiness is as important to you as your own. When you love to be with him. When you feel complete within yourself but even better when you're with that person."

"I just wish Crumpet were a man—"

"You're going to have to look for the two-legged variety, Rosalind. I want you to be happy."

"But I *am*."

"You'll be happier. Trust me."

She was brought back to the present by her mother's tone. "Rosalind? Rosalind? Have you heard a word I've said?"

She blinked her eyes. "Of course, Mother."

"Then it's all right?"

Knowing her mother would bulldoze her until she gave in, Roz acquiesced gracefully.

"I *knew* I could count on you! Harold will be so thrilled. Now, I thought we could have an arch of roses at the end of the garden, and I could walk down those stone steps. We could serve a buffet out by the pool, and then Harold and I could borrow the Rolls and leave for the airport in style!''

"The wedding? You want to have it here?" Roz felt as if she were underwater, trying to swim to the surface.

"That's what we were talking about! Rosalind, were you listening?"

She pressed her fingers against her temples. "I'm sorry, Mother. I'm just tired."

"If you didn't work so hard with those animals. They don't pay you enough, anyway—"

"Mother." Roz forced her tone to be bright. "Why don't you and I get dressed up and go out to dinner tonight? I know this great Chinese place. Wouldn't that be fun?"

"You were always bright in school. I never understood why you didn't finish and go on to college. You had such potential—"

"Mother. Chinese food?"

Deena smiled, and Roz noticed there were more fine lines around her nose and mouth. Her green eyes, so like her own, looked worried. Maybe her mother wasn't as sure of this marriage as she said she was.

"We could get that shrimp in lobster sauce you always liked."

Deena surprised her then, reaching across the table and grasping her hand tightly. "I'd like that, Rosalind."

THEY ENDED UP getting Chinese for three to go. Jesse had an acting class, and Deena insisted on not leaving Jamie out. Roz didn't want to leave the new dog alone for long, so they ate in her bedroom. She ordered some plain strips of beef, along with several other entrées, and before she ate anything, she coaxed the setter to eat.

Jamie recognized her mood and was happy for her. The setter, though literally almost dead, had responded and eaten some of the beef. Crumpet stood quivering in the wings, and Roz finally took pity and gave him the rest of the beef with a little bit of lobster sauce.

"But only because you've lost so much weight."

"Careful," Jamie said. "You don't want him to think of food as a reward. Perhaps we could interest Crumpet in a hobby instead."

Even Deena smiled at that one. But Roz laughed, then gave him a smile that was all he could have hoped for.

He was fascinated, watching her with her mother. Theirs was a relationship that had many dimensions, but the one that struck him most forcibly was their role reversal. Deena seemed unsure of herself at times and asked Rosalind for approval in so many silent ways. She also seemed to need to maintain a subtle competition with her daughter. He was surprised to see these remarks slide off Roz. She seemed to be protecting her mother.

They talked about the wedding, and Jamie volunteered his services. Deena was clearly enchanted with him, and he caught her sending several speculative glances between the two of them. Later in the evening, she stopped being so subtle.

"Have you ever eaten one of Rosalind's omelets? She's quite a good cook." Deena leaned back on her elbows against the carpeted floor and studied him intently.

Jamie, catching Roz's embarrassed expression, sailed right into the conversation and attempted to defuse Deena. "We're both pretty terrible about cooking at home. I think it's people like Roz and me that keep the fast-food chains in business."

"She does work very hard." Deena sent a glance at her daughter. "I worry about her. I've been hoping she'll find the right man, settle down and start a family."

"Mother!"

He noticed Roz's face beginning to turn red and patted Deena's hand reassuringly. "She has quite a family already, and they all adore her. Has she given you a tour of the stable area yet?"

"I'm sure it's filled to the brim with animals." Deena's tone made Jamie suspect she wasn't pleased by this. "I just don't understand why Roz hasn't settled down. She used to date all the time when she was in high school. The phone was constantly ringing—"

"Mother, that's enough."

"Rosalind, don't be upset with me! I'm just telling Jamie little family things—nothing to get upset about."

"I'd rather you wouldn't."

Deena turned one of her most dazzling smiles on Jamie, and he felt his stomach begin to tighten. He had to think of a way to end Roz's discomfort.

"She was one of the prettiest, most popular girls in her graduating class. When she went to the prom, I remember thinking she looked so—"

"I have to check on the rest of the animals." Abruptly, Roz stood up and walked out of the bedroom.

Deena stared after her. "I don't know why she's so touchy." She looked up at Jamie. "You do like Rosalind, don't you, Jamie?"

"We're good friends, Deena."

"Oh." She seemed disappointed, and Jamie had to resist the urge to tell her how deeply she was embarrassing—and alienating—her daughter.

"Let me show you the room Roz fixed for you."

"Oh, no." She stood up and dusted off the skirt. Then she located her pumps and wiggled her feet into them. "Harold is going to pick me up; then we're going out for a drink. I just had to make sure it was all right with my daughter if we had the wedding here. He should be here any minute. Would you walk me to the front door? This place is so big, I might get lost."

Harold was a complete surprise. At least fifteen years Deena's junior, he was deeply tanned and sported longish hair and an ear cuff. His faded jeans clung tightly to his well-muscled legs, and his black tank top showed off impressive biceps. Jamie watched Deena's entire expression change as she gazed up into his face. She became softer, more girlish. Her eyes were totally adoring.

"Ready to go?" Harold was a man of few words.

"All set." Deena turned to Jamie. "Would you tell Rosalind I'll be back Wednesday with a list of things we have to get done?"

"I will, Deena. Nice meeting you. You too, Harold—" They were already halfway down the long, circular drive. Jamie stared after them for a few minutes, then smiled as he heard a motorcycle being revved.

Then he carefully locked the door and walked down the hall in search of Rosalind.

SHE WAS SITTING on the cement floor of one of the runs, watching several kittens of assorted shapes and sizes attack the giant pan of food she had just set down. As they ate, she ran her hands through their fur and scratched their ears. Several of them were half wild, and she had to get them used to being touched. They had to learn to associate good things with human contact.

Jamie was standing in the shadows, watching her. She had been aware of his presence when he first stood in the doorway, but she didn't acknowledge him. Her mind was working furiously, wondering what she was going to do.

She liked Jamie. She didn't want to lie to him. If her mother hadn't opened her mouth tonight, she would never have had to say anything. But Deena had done her usual job of telling things as she wanted them to be rather than as they actually were. And she couldn't let Jamie believe something that wasn't true. She hated people with false images, and she didn't want to have one.

She worked her way slowly through the line of runs, carrying pans of food and petting the various animals. Some were still frightened and scurried into corners as she unlocked their cages. She let them be, knowing they would come to her when they were ready.

Later, as she was washing out several of the bowls in the large sink, she heard Jamie approach.

"Your mother left."

"Did she say where she was going?"

"Harold picked her up."

"So how's husband number seven?" she asked sarcastically. She knew she sounded cruel, but she was still upset by her mother's lies.

"He seemed like a nice guy."

She rinsed the last bowl and stacked it by the sink, then quickly dried her hands. "You left Crumpet alone in the bedroom?"

"I let him finish the fried rice, then turned on the television. *Top Hat* was just coming on the movie channel."

"That should amuse him. He likes Fred Astaire."

She could feel him watching her as she turned off the lights and secured the stable for the night. Then, as she began to walk toward the mansion's lighted windows, he followed her. But instead of going directly inside, she stopped by the pool and sat down in one of the wrought-iron chairs.

"There's something I have to tell you, Jamie."

"You don't have to tell me anything." He sat down next to her.

"No, I want to tell you. The last thing I'd want is for you to believe something that isn't true."

He was silent then, and she wondered what he was thinking.

She tilted her head back and looked up at the night sky.

"I'm an okay cook, but nothing special."

"Roz—"

"I never dated in high school. The phones didn't ring. I dropped out of school in the ninth grade and never went back. I was never popular, and I never went to a prom. Okay?"

"It doesn't make any difference to me. I don't care about things like that."

"But I wanted you to *know*."

They were both silent, and Roz took a deep breath, then held it, trying to ease the tightness in her chest. What had she hoped to accomplish by telling Jamie the truth?

"And my mother is a liar. She tells things to suit whoever she's with. She's always had this obsession with wanting to move up in the world, so she always told people we had more money than we did, that I was smarter than I was." She took a deep breath. "I hated school, Jamie. I always wanted to be outside doing things. The only thing I liked to do—still like to do—is read."

"You've always struck me as an intelligent person."

"She always tried to marry money," Roz said softly. "And it never worked. I must have lived in over twenty-five houses by the time I was thirteen. We were always moving." She stopped talking as soon as her voice started to tremble. Jamie didn't move, didn't speak, so she just sat quietly, regaining her composure.

"She was never home. I used to watch movies all the time so I wouldn't feel so alone. All my life I've wondered what the other side of the screen would be like. They were really my family." She cleared her throat.

"You know what I wanted more than anything when I was a little kid?"

"What?"

"I wanted to sit down at a table with my mother and have dinner together. I wanted us to talk and laugh like those stupid sitcoms on television. But we never did. Most of the time we ate in front of the television, or she left me money to go to the store and get something. I remember I ate at a friend's house once. I never had so much fun. I just wanted to feel like a family."

"I know she loves you, Roz. She cares about you."

"I know. And I'm not asking for your pity. My mother worked hard; she sacrificed a lot for me. But sometimes I felt like—you know the type of people who get a puppy and then when it gets big and it's not cute anymore, they take it out in the car and dump it?"

Jamie nodded.

"Well, my mother never dumped me, but I felt like that. I felt like once I wasn't cute anymore, once I wasn't a baby and still needed so much from her, she just didn't have the time, didn't want to give it to me."

He was silent, and for one agonizing moment Roz was horrified she had told him so much. The only other person she had confided in was Matthew. And he hadn't been an emotional threat.

"Maybe not didn't want. Maybe just not capable."

His words were so soft she wasn't sure she'd heard him correctly. Something deep inside, something frozen and tight, began to melt, break apart. Roz ducked her head so her hair swept over her cheek, hiding her face from his view.

She felt his fingers close over hers. His hand was warm, but she forced her fingers to remain lifeless, resisting the temptation to hold on to him, to feel connected.

"You're a very lovable person, Roz. I hope you know that."

His words started to make her stomach come apart. Her eyes swam with tears of frustration and weariness. Standing up, she tried to walk past him, but his body was blocking hers. She tried to evade him one more time, but he caught her gently in his arms and pulled her against the warmth and hardness of his body.

"I think you need a hug," he said softly.

It was wonderful, being held in his arms. They came around her, and rather than feeling suffocated or trapped, she felt enclosed in pure warmth. She felt his hands come up over her back, and just the touch of his fingers seemed to melt away some of the tension. Her hands groped clumsily, then reached around his waist and clasped him tightly against her. He smelled of soap, and his clothes felt soft. Roz closed her eyes and held him briefly, then released him.

He didn't let go.

His chin rested on top of her hair; his arms were still warm and secure. Not knowing quite what to do, Roz hugged him again. More than anything, she simply wanted to melt into him, to be close. She tried, tentatively. She leaned slightly, felt his body balance again, catch and hold her. Then her body surprised her, beginning to shake. He held her tighter; then it seemed as if she were falling apart. Her stomach trembled;

long-repressed tears sprang into her eyes and began to roll swiftly down her face.

"Oh, Roz." She felt Jamie's body shifting; then he was slowly sitting down in one of the chairs and easing her into his lap. She curled up against him, her face pressed against his chest, and sobbed.

It was a combination of everything. Matthew. Crumpet. Her mother and all her lies. The past. Everything she had ever been afraid of. And a part of it felt so right, to sit in this man's lap and let him hold her while she cried her heart out.

Afterward, he pulled a handkerchief out of his jeans pocket, and she blew her nose. He kissed her cheek, then smiled and hoisted her up into his arms.

Roz panicked, and as tired as she was, she felt her body tense. What now? She didn't have a great deal of experience with men, and she wasn't sure what to do. She liked Jamie, cared for him. But it was too soon, too soon . . .

"Don't be frightened. Nothing's going to happen to you. I'm going to take care of you." She heard the whispered words and relaxed against his chest as he began to walk toward the mansion.

He carried her up to her room, then pulled back the covers and helped her unfasten her jeans. Roz couldn't remember ever feeling so exhausted in her life. She was beyond modesty. And besides, hadn't he undressed her before?

She felt the mattress shift as he sat down next to her, and she reached tiredly for his hand.

"She wipes me out."

"Your mother?"

Roz nodded her head. The effort felt enormous, but she knew it was the slightest of nods.

"I'll help you through the wedding, Roz. If you'll let me." He pulled the covers over her and tucked her into bed.

"Okay." Her voice sounded high and faint, thin.

"You sleep now. I'll wake you up in the morning."

"But the dog—"

"There's more beef and some baby food in the cupboard. I'll see she eats something."

"Crumpet—"

"Crumpet will be fine."

She smiled then and slowly turned over on her stomach, careful to keep holding his hand. Almost a minute passed, and Roz could feel herself beginning to fall asleep.

"Jamie?"

"Hmm?"

"Thank you."

"No problem. Hugs are my specialty."

"I always wanted one just like that. It was perfect."

"What do you mean?"

She was fighting sleep, but she had to tell him. She'd be too scared in the morning. "I always wanted to be hugged and not be the last one to let go. You know what I mean?"

"Yeah, I know exactly."

"You do? You really do?"

"I do. You sleep tight, Roz. I'll see you in the morning."

She felt him lean over and kiss the top of her head, then her cheek. She let go of his hand and listened as his footsteps faded quietly away.

HE STAYED AWAKE almost all night. The setter in the bathroom ate some chicken baby food. Crumpet practically sat in his lap until he offered a taste to him, too. And later he sat in the doorway, one eye on the Irish setter, the other on Roz.

There was absolutely no way a woman who respected life so much would have killed Matthew Barrett. His fingers itched, and Jamie knew he was anxious, wanted to start smoking again. One piece of the puzzle behind the old man's death had fallen into place. One person was out of the running.

He listened to his instincts, having honed them well in his business. And if he wasn't sure of anything else, he was sure of two things.

Rosalind Locklear was no murderess.

Matthew Barrett had been murdered.

And that led to his final conclusion, the thought that wouldn't let him sleep.

The murderer was still at large.

Chapter Five

"He's interested in you."

"Oh, Mother, be serious! You came over today to discuss your wedding, not Jamie. There's too much that has to be done. Do you want red roses or yellow? I like the apricot; they would look beautiful against your—"

"I can see it in the way he looks at you."

"Mother! Will you *stop*? Jamie and I are just friends. Nothing more. Now let's get back to the list. Please." The last thing Rosalind wanted her mother to suspect was that there was any strong feeling between her and Jamie. Deena had never been subtle, and she wasn't about to change her ways now. The feelings Roz was beginning to have for Jamie were too tender, too tentative, to share with anyone. All of this was new to her, and she wanted to hide it from her mother, keep it to herself and cherish it a little while longer.

"All I can say, darling, is if I had a man so charming and handsome under my roof, I wouldn't waste any time. I'd let him know I was interested."

"Mother, I *know* what you'd do. When are you going to accept that you and I have totally different styles of operating?"

"So you *are* interested."

"No. I did *not* say that. I said we were different. Do you want the red, the yellow or the apricot?"

"You really like the apricot?"

"They'd look beautiful with your gown."

Deena gave her daughter a long, assessing look. "Darling, I knew you were the perfect person to help me with this! I'd still be on the first question. I'm so proud of you."

Despite her guard, Roz felt the beginnings of a small flare of pride welling up inside her. "Thank you, Mother. We still have the last third of this list to get through. Sit-down or buffet?"

SINCE THE NIGHT BY THE POOL, when Rosalind had been so brutally honest with him, Jamie had been finding it more and more difficult to hide his real identity from her.

A butler. She thinks you're a butler. What would she do if she knew your real reason for being here? She was a woman who would have to trust a man, respect him, before she came to love him.

And at the moment he didn't respect himself very much for lying to her. But it wasn't possible for him to tell her the entire truth. Not yet. She was under enough pressure, and he was sure Roz had no idea Matthew had been murdered. That was information the police had agreed to keep quiet.

It was information no one would have had to begin with if Jamie's mother hadn't flown in one of the country's top coroners. Someone had been slowly drugging Matthew, and his death had been made to look like a heart attack. The first inkling of foul play had come when Meryl Cameron had declared that Matthew Barrett was as healthy as a horse and there wasn't any history of heart trouble in his entire family. Jamie and his mother had managed to keep his murder a secret, not wanting it plastered all over every tabloid in town. They wanted to catch the killer unaware.

But then why would anyone be going after Crumpet? What would they have to gain? It didn't make sense. Matthew had made his will airtight. If something happened to Crumpet, or in the event the bulldog died of natural causes, Matthew's fortune was to be turned over to animal-protection agencies. None of his children were going to get anything. Matt, Sarah and Elizabeth had been the obvious suspects. But if all three of them had nothing to gain, why would they try to kill the dog? They were busy enough trying to contest the original will and claim more of their father's wealth.

The most interesting thing about Matthew's will was the trust fund he had set up for his grandson, Mark. When the boy reached the age of twenty-five, he would receive a third. At thirty, another third. The last third would be given to him on his thirty-fifth birthday. He was the only one of Matthew's relatives who had received a substantial sum of money. And Jamie knew Sarah had been pleased by the trust fund. Whatever else he thought about Matthew's three children, Sarah was a vigilant mother. Perhaps a little too much.

He sighed and sat up in bed. Roz and her mother were out by the pool, discussing wedding details. He didn't know how Roz had so much patience with Deena. The woman would have driven him absolutely insane within thirty minutes. But there it was again, that peculiar mother-daughter role reversal. Deena seemed calmer, less frantic, now that Roz was handling the details.

You just have to be patient and wait for the killer to reveal himself. It was an old police truism that if the killer wasn't caught within forty-eight hours after the murder, he usually went free. But this was a different sort of case. He had an intensely personal stake in Matthew Barrett's murder. Jamie's mother and Matthew had known each other since he and her older brother had gone to college together. Matthew had always felt close to the entire Cameron family, especially Meryl. She bred English bulldogs and had given Crumpet to Matthew when the bulldog was eight weeks old. Matthew had been enchanted with the puppy from the moment he'd seen him and had planned on getting a female. He and Meryl had spent hours talking on the phone, going over proper diet and care. And training! Jamie grinned as he remembered his mother's frustration at the way Matthew spoiled Crumpet. "Outrageous. Outrageous what he lets that bulldog get away with. The first thing I'd do is put that animal on a rigid diet and get those excess pounds off."

Mom would just love Roz. He had thought that many times as he'd watched her work with the animals. And he'd wondered if he would still be friends with her after this case was completed. Like it or not,

Rosalind was caught up in the middle of it. Everything had to continue as it had since Matthew's death in order for the killer to be caught. Patience was what was needed. Patience and skill.

When Jamie wasn't around the house, other investigators watched the mansion, contacting him if anyone came near the estate. When he managed to get away, it was to find out as much as he could about the Barrett family. It had been slow going. They were a closely knit group.

Especially since Matthew's death.

And Matthew had had many enemies. He had been an amazing businessman in his earlier years, and intense jealousy from others was to be expected in the life of anyone so successful. But jealous enough to kill! Who would have profited from Matthew's death?

The billion-dollar question. Literally. He glanced down at the clock by his bed. At noon, he had offered to give Roz a ride to the shelter. Crumpet would ride in the car with them and stay with him until Roz finished her shift. Then he would pick her up. Maybe he'd rent a few videos. Maybe a musical, so that Crumpet could be entertained and they could talk.

She'd been shy with him after that evening by the pool, scrupulously careful not to reveal any further emotions. And he had been saddened by that, because he knew she still didn't trust him. Though he managed to eat most meals with her—and he knew she was touched by his having remembered her childhood wish—she seemed to maintain an invisible wall between them.

He glanced at the clock again and thought quickly. If he went out by the pool now, he could make sure

Roz made it to the shelter on time so Deena wouldn't talk her into doing more work than they had agreed upon. But then he had to endure Deena. But if he didn't, he knew Roz wouldn't put up a fight. She'd be too tired after several hours with her mother.

He thought of Roz. Of the shadows beneath her eyes. The way sometimes at dinner she would look so tired. She had put in many hours with the Irish setter she had been so determined to save. Tentatively christened Rocky, the dog was a complete emotional mess, wetting the floor whenever anyone approached her, quivering with fear until Roz put her arms around her and talked to her.

"Why Rocky?" he had asked her one night.

"She's a fighter. She's going to last until the final round."

The setter remained in the bathroom, scared of everyone and everything. Whenever she saw him, her tail would whip between her legs, and she would half walk, half crawl, until she was in the far corner of the bathroom. Then she would curl up on the tiles and try to become invisible.

Roz was overextended; there was no question about that. He had talked her into hiring another of Jesse's siblings, his sixteen-year-old brother, and Raphael worked with the animals part-time.

Still, Roz always looked tired.

There was no question in his mind. He couldn't let her face Deena alone. With a sigh of resignation, he made sure his gun and shoulder holster were safely hidden, then closed his bedroom door after him and walked down the marble hall toward the backyard.

HE DROVE ROZ'S TOYOTA to the shelter. Crumpet sat in the middle of the front seat, over the parking brake. The bulldog leaned against Roz's arm, then crawled into her lap and stuck his head out the window. His ears perked up, and he started to bark as he caught sight of a poodle in a red Corvette.

"That guy never quits," Jamie said, shifting into third.

"I think he's been bored lately," Roz confessed, threading her fingers through Crumpet's leather collar. "Matthew used to baby him outrageously. He didn't have other animals to take care of."

"Crumpet and I will take a spin once we drop you off, get some fast food. How about El Pollo Loco, Crump?"

Crumpet barked at the poodle again. The Corvette was ahead of them, and the bulldog reared up on his hind legs and tried to lean his upper body out the car window.

"That's it, Crumpet." Roz pulled him gently back into her lap and rolled up the window. "Make sure to keep this window up or he'll jump out."

"He wouldn't have to jump. He'd fall." Even though Crumpet had slimmed down considerably, he was still top-heavy.

She smiled. "Just keep the window rolled up and watch out for dogs."

He cleared his throat, cursing himself for feeling as nervous as a virgin. "Roz, I was wondering if one night we might go out for dinner."

"We have dinner together every night."

She didn't understand. "No, I meant—you know, you and I. Like a date."

"A date?" She sounded confused.

"You know. I ask you; you accept. We both get dressed up, only instead of driving to your house, I'd simply walk down the hall and pick you up."

"You and I? A date?" She was beginning to sound like a broken record.

"Roz, I like you. I think you like me—"

"Of course I like you."

"Well, people who like each other generally go out."

"But I thought we were friends."

"We are friends. I just thought you might like to go out. Get out of the house. See something different."

"Oh. Oh. I thought you meant like a *real* date. I didn't understand what you meant."

He parked the car in front of the shelter and reached over to hold Crumpet by the collar. "That's not what I meant. I meant like a real date. Like someone asking someone out because he really likes her and wants to get to know her better."

Dead silence. Roz looked away, out the window.

"I like you, Roz. A lot. I'd like to start seeing you." The expression sounded totally out-of-date, but he didn't know how else to say it.

She was quiet for so long, he didn't know what to say. But she didn't jump out of the car and run. That had to mean something.

"Oh, Jamie." Her words came out on the softest sigh. "I never meant for this to happen."

"I didn't either. Not when I first applied. I was only here to do a job."

"I do like you."

He waited. He had already put his feelings on the line. He had to know how she felt.

"I like you as much as I've ever liked anyone. I just don't know if I want to get involved right now."

Such safe words. He knew they covered up a multitude of fears. Roz didn't have a great deal of social experience; she had told him that once over one of their dinners. Suddenly he was frightened. Why couldn't he have left things alone? He could have continued having dinner with her most nights without risking an emotional confrontation like this one.

Be honest with her. At least in the areas you can be. He had revealed his feelings to her; there was no turning back.

"Can I ask you again later?"

"If you still want to. Jamie, it's nothing against you. You're a wonderful person. It's me. I don't feel ready right now. Maybe never."

She needed more time. At least she hadn't decided to fire him. If he continued on the way they had been together, winning her trust, maybe she would consider a date. All he could do was be a friend and try to help her believe a relationship might be possible.

If nothing else, he was certainly patient.

"Okay. I won't make this a bigger deal than it is. I like you, Roz, and I'm not going to hide my feelings."

"I *do* like you, Jamie." He could tell the words were an effort for her. "If I wanted a relationship with anyone, it would be you. But can we just drop it for now? Please?"

There's too much in her life. Don't press.

"Sure. Have a good day."

"Thanks." She petted Crumpet's head. "Be a good dog and don't make any trouble. Okay, boy?" Then she touched Jamie's arm gently. For a moment it seemed she was going to say something, but then she opened the door and got out.

He watched her until she disappeared into the squat stucco building.

THE MORNING OF DEENA'S WEDDING was cool and clear. It was a Saturday in early October, Indian summer at its best. When Roz went out to feed the animals, she glanced up at the sky and smiled.

She and her mother had reached another plateau. Their typical pattern was to spend time away from each other, then come together for an intense, brief period, usually when Deena needed something organized in her life. Her wedding had been no exception.

But this was different. After Matthew had died, Roz had spent time alone, trying to decide what it was she really wanted to do with her life. She had also reassessed her worth as a human being. After all, Matthew had trusted her with his most precious possession—Crumpet.

The object of her thoughts dogged her heels, snorting. She had already measured out his breakfast and taken him for his morning run. Some mornings Crumpet would race up the stairs and try to climb back into bed with Jesse. He was working nights, acting in a one-act play in an equity-waiver theater in Hollywood, so another one of his brothers, Pablo, was the new chauffeur. On other mornings, Crumpet would join Jamie on his run, then come racing back inside and collapse on the rug in front of the kitchen fireplace. But today he was with Roz.

Though Crumpet still followed her around and was clearly her devoted dog, she was glad he was beginning to respond to other people. She had been heartbroken at the sight of Crumpet after Matthew's death. The dog had waited by the front door for over a week as if he expected Matthew to walk in the door. And how could she have faulted Crumpet when she had wanted to believe the same thing herself? Then the bulldog had gone through a very depressed time, eating little and sleeping constantly.

But you went on living, just like I did. She gave Crumpet a quick pat between kennel runs, then continued methodically down the line, making sure each animal was fed.

When she finished, she swept out the front of the stable, then cleaned several cages. Finally done, she snapped her fingers, and Crumpet came bounding up to her. He had been sniffing around the front of the stable by the flower beds, looking for butterflies. Crumpet never gave up, even though he never caught any. But they fascinated him, and Roz laughed every time the dog caught sight of a butterfly. His eyes became intense, and he stood perfectly still; then he rushed clumsily in and attempted to bite it. But it always got away.

"Don't look so happy, Crump. It's my turn for breakfast. You've had yours." When he butted his head against one of her legs, she had to laugh. "Maybe a piece of bacon. I'm proud of you, Crumpet, holding your new weight. You look beautiful, but you know that, huh?"

They raced back to the kitchen, Crumpet barking all the way. As Roz opened the door and let herself in, she stopped. Jamie was standing by the sink, finishing the last of a bowl of cereal. He was dressed in faded jeans, a black T-shirt and running shoes. He looked tired and discouraged.

"Hi." Though she had been slightly unnerved when Jamie had asked her out, Roz had tried her best not to act strangely when they ran into each other. She just made sure those moments weren't frequent. In a mansion the size of Matthew's, it was easy to avoid someone. But it wasn't possible all the time. So she tried to avoid being shy and self-centered and always made an effort to act normally.

"Hi." He quickly washed the bowl and spoon, then set them in the dish drain to dry. "I'm running some errands this morning. Do you need anything?"

"I think we're all set. The florists should be here any minute with the arch; the food's arriving later in the afternoon. Everything should be set up by five." Deena had opted for a ceremony close to sunset, then a huge buffet and a band out on the back terrace.

"When does your mom get here?"

"She'll blow in at the last minute. It used to drive me crazy, but now I just expect it." When he didn't reply, Roz began to assemble fruit for her breakfast shake. There were so many times she wished she and Jamie could have remained the simple friends they had been. But her instincts had warned her. Even the night he had held her out by the pool, she had known their friendship was blossoming into something different. The tiniest amounts of tension had begun to weave their way into their daily routine. Awareness was heightened, every move and word measured and considered before it was performed.

The phone rang, startling her as she sliced the banana into the blender. Wiping her hands on her gray sweatpants, Roz picked up the receiver.

"Can I speak to T.J.?" The voice was soft and feminine, with a hint of laughter in it.

"T.J.? I think you have—" The she caught sight of Jamie gesturing. Putting her hand over the mouthpiece, she said, "Do you know a T.J.?"

"It's for me."

"Do you want me to leave?" She had the oddest sensation in the pit of her stomach at the thought of the female on the other end of the line, talking to Jamie.

"No problem. Finish your shake."

She couldn't help overhearing parts of the conversation, but it was the general tone that filled her with a crazy sort of despair. Jamie was relaxed as he leaned against the wall, laughing and joking. His discouraged mood seemed to have lifted; he seemed more alive. Roz continued cutting up fruit, then emptied a carton of low-fat yogurt into the blender. Crumpet, not a fruit-and-yogurt fan, was lying sprawled out on the Mexican tile, intently watching the small black-and-white television on the counter.

"No, I'm okay. Nothing new. You did what? Are you kidding?" He laughed then, and though Roz loved to hear him laugh, she wondered who it was that inspired such obvious joy in Jamie.

"Sure, I'll talk to her." Roz gritted her teeth as she tried not to listen to the one-sided conversation. What did Jamie have, a whole harem of women waiting for him? How could she have been so naive as to think he would wait for her to make up her mind? *He asked you to go out to dinner with him, not marry him. Just an evening of each other's company and you froze up. A social retard, that's what you are.* She punched the blender button with a vengeance and watched as the yogurt and fruit blended into a thick health shake. As the motor whirred, she added honey, wheat germ and the smallest amount of brewer's yeast.

Turning off the blender, she heard the tail end of a sentence.

"—I love you, too. I think I may be able to get away in another week."

Get away. So that's how he looks at you now, since you were so rude to him. A simple dinner. That's all he wanted. He might have even gone out with you a few times and decided he didn't want to date you anymore. Oh, Roz, grow up!

He hung up the phone and was almost out the kitchen door before Roz asked the question that wanted to explode out.

"Who was that on the phone?" *Good. You got just the right amount of casual interest in your tone.* He looked so very happy, and even though she was glad his earlier discouragement had left him, she was startled to find she was the tiniest bit jealous of the woman who could have such an effect on him.

"My sister. Then my mom."

"Your *mother*? You talk like that to your mother?" The words were out before she could think about how they must have sounded.

"What do you mean? How should I talk with my mom?"

"You sounded like best friends."

"We are. I consider her one of my friends. As well as my mother."

The idea was completely foreign to her. Suddenly she realized how little information Jamie had ever volunteered about himself. And it wasn't that she hadn't asked him. But he had a real knack of turning the questioning back to her and letting his own life remain a mystery.

"Your sister? How many brothers and sisters do you have?" This time she was going to remain alert and not let him change the subject.

"I have an older brother and two younger sisters."

"Where does everyone live?"

"In San Francisco."

"What does your dad do?"

"He's a writer." Jamie looked sheepish for just an instant, and Roz suddenly had the feeling he didn't mean someone who occasionally sent out an article.

"What does he write?"

"Mysteries."

"What's his name?"

When he named one of her favorite authors, she could only stare at him. When she finally found her voice again, she said, "He's one of my favorites. Matthew's, too. He gave me an autographed copy once, and that started me. I've read all his books, both series. The one about the detective, and the other one, with the woman who breeds dogs. Oh, Jamie, tell your father he gave Matthew so much pleasure! He used to buy his books the minute they came out!"

"I'll let him know that." Now he really did look sheepish.

"And your mom? She must be someone very special if you can talk to her like that."

"She is."

"Was it—was it fun growing up with your brother and sisters?" She flashed to a quick mental image of Jamie as he must have looked as a boy, surrounded by a loving family.

"It had its moments." He looked as if he wanted to edge out the door, and Roz realized she had been interrogating him for several minutes. Maybe it was making him uncomfortable.

"I'm sorry, Jamie. I didn't mean to get so nosy."

"It didn't bother me." But she had the strangest feeling that it had.

"I have one more question; then I'll let you go."

"Shoot."

"What does the *T* stand for?"

For the slightest moment, a pained expression passed across his face; then his features were quickly composed. "I'd rather not say."

"Why?"

"I never liked the name. Everyone has always called me Jamie."

Before she could reply, he asked, "How did your mother think up the name Rosalind? Is it a family name?"

Roz thought quickly. *A family name.* Her family seemed pathetic after this brief glimpse of Jamie's. Deena had been thrown out of her parents' house when they discovered she was pregnant. She had never married Roz's father. He hadn't cared to stick around. So her mother was the only family Roz had ever known.

"No, it's not a family name. My mother thought it was pretty. She—she got it out of a historical romance she was reading when she was pregnant with me."

"It's a beautiful name." His tone was slightly softer, and something inside her yearned to respond.

"I hate it. It was so different. When I was little, I always wanted to be named something like Susan or Anne. But I can live with Roz."

"It suits you." He leaned in the doorway, arms crossed in front of his chest, and Roz was struck by the fact that he didn't seem in a hurry anymore. "It's different and romantic and sensual."

"It doesn't suit me at all. I'm not romantic; I don't believe in all that stuff."

"You don't?" The question was so gentle. She was surprised to find her eyes stinging.

"No."

"Come to dinner with me, Roz." His blue eyes were intense, his gaze never leaving her face. "Let that other person out. See if you like her."

Curiously, she knew exactly what he meant. It frightened her, knowing he had watched her for so long and knew parts of what was inside her. Yet she knew he would never take advantage of her or use his knowledge in a hurtful way. There was nothing egotistical or power-seeking in his assessment. He was simply telling her the truth.

"I—I'd like to." She forced her answer out past a very tight throat. "I'd like that a lot." He smiled, but she put her hand up in front of her as if to keep him away from her. "But don't expect a lot from me, Jamie. We're different people. I—I don't have a lot of experience going out. You may find me—''

"I find you absolutely wonderful." He surprised her then, walking straight up to her and catching her around the waist. His eyes were incredibly blue for just an instant before he lowered his head and touched his lips gently to hers. Roz stood perfectly still, frightened. Awkward. His lips were warm and firm, his arms solid around her waist. One hand slid up her neck and briefly cradled the back of her head, threading his fingers through her hair.

As quickly as his lips touched hers, they left. She looked up at his face, anxious about what she would see. But it was simply Jamie. His eyes were alive, his mouth soft. She wondered if hers looked the same. She felt softer somehow, as if some of the tension had left her body. With a start, she realized she was leaning into him, and she shifted the balance of her body so she was standing slightly apart.

"Why did you do that?"

"Did you like it?"

"Why?" she persisted.

He cupped her face in his hands, his thumbs caressing her cheekbones. "I look at it this way, Roz. The entire time we'd be out trying to have a good time, we'd both be nervous about that kiss. You'd be wondering if I was going to kiss you. I'd be worried about when I should do it. So the way I figure it, the thing to do is to kiss at unsuspecting moments so that neither one of us has a chance to get nervous."

"Are you serious?"

"No, I just wanted to kiss you. Did you mind?"

She could feel herself blushing. "No." She didn't want to be frightened of Jamie, of the new feelings he was beginning to make her aware of. She wanted to be honest with him. And she was surprised to find she wanted to be closer to him.

"Good." He pressed one of his fingers gently to her lips, then ran it lightly over her lower lip. "I have to go."

She felt strangely bereft, knowing he was going to walk out the door. She was surprised to find she wanted him to kiss her again. As soon as she thought about it, he must have seen her eyes, for his expression changed. She saw something flare up in his eyes; then he was slowly lowering his face to hers. She lifted her chin, and a strange, wild excitement began to race through her body as she realized this time she was going to kiss him back.

At the exact instant before their lips met, Crumpet exploded into action. He jumped up and began to bark furiously, then lunged at the black-and-white TV, knocking it to the other side of the counter, where it teetered precariously.

"What the—" Jamie jerked away from her as if Crumpet had gone for his leg.

"Change the channel! There's a dog on the set!" Roz tackled Crumpet and groped for his collar. The bulldog was quivering in fury, yapping excitedly. As Lorne Greene's familiar voice began to fill the kitchen, Jamie reached over and flipped the switch. Another early-morning program. The newscaster's voice was pleasant and well modulated. Roz felt Crumpet relax beneath her hands, and after one or two soft snarls, he stretched out and began to watch the program.

Roz couldn't meet Jamie's eyes. She was horrified to find laughter rising inside her throat. Her stomach was beginning to cramp with the effort of holding it in. But she had to see what he was feeling. When their eyes met, she was astonished to see laughter in his own.

"Hey, do I know how to pick moments, or do I know how to pick moments?"

She started to laugh. He sunk down onto the tile with her, and she laughed until she was crying.

"Have you thought about flying Crumpet to New York? He could do that on David Letterman's show."

She could hardly talk; her stomach was cramping so badly, it hurt to breathe. "There was a dog on that already did that. I was watching it, but Crumpet— Crumpet attacked the screen, and I had to turn it off."

That sent them into gales of hilarity again, and they held on to each other. Crumpet, thinking this was an incredibly fun new game, raced around them in circles, yapping and yapping.

Roz was wiping her eyes and smiling at Jamie when she heard tapping at the kitchen door. She looked up and watched as her mother walked in, holding her ivory silk dress in plastic.

Deena took in the entire room, then slowly smiled.

THE WEDDING WAS, out of Deena's seven marriages, the best. She had eloped three times and had three other ceremonies, but Roz wanted to think of this one as the last. Harold and Deena stood under the rose-decorated arch and recited their vows. Roz was maid of honor, and a friend of Harold's, named Eddie, was best man. Eddie had hair that was longer than Harold's, but both of them looked surprisingly hand-some in their suits. Deena wore a simple silk dress, and her bouquet of lilies, roses and baby's breath was ab-solutely stunning. Roz wore her hair up, and her dress was a very pale shade of peach.

She knew Jamie was somewhere among the guests; her mother had insisted on inviting him. "Who knows; he might start getting ideas." Roz prayed her mother wouldn't say anything embarrassing to Jamie at the reception.

During the ceremony, Roz's thoughts drifted. She had been surprised by how serious Deena and Harold were taking all this. After all, when someone had been married seven times, how serious could marriage vows be? But there was something in her mother's expres-sion this time that touched her deeply. Deena looked a little older this visit. Roz never asked her mother about her life when she didn't see her regularly. And this time, with her mother looking more careworn than she had in the past, she had no desire to know. But she was moved by the way Deena looked up into Harold's eyes, the way her voice quivered when she promised to love, honor and cherish—Deena would never obey.

Afterward, during the buffet, Roz had her first glimpse of Jamie. He had arrived late, when the cer-emony had been almost ready to begin and Roz had been calming her mother down. Now, as she walked over to the buffet table, she noticed him. He was dressed in a beautifully cut charcoal-gray suit. Crum-pet was by his side, on a short leather lead, a peach ribbon around his neck.

"I thought you two should match." Jamie had taken Crumpet with him on his errands so that Roz would be free to help her mother.

"Where did you get that bow?" Crumpet looked like a large white present wearing the intricate shiny bow.

"I stopped by the florist on the way home. When I told them what I needed and they knew I was coming to this wedding, they gave me this." His gaze skimmed quickly over her. "You look great, Roz. Just like a peach."

"I hope that wasn't a reference to my weight." Roz reached out and picked up a paper plate. Deena had decided to go informal.

"The only one here who'll ever have to worry about that is our furry friend in the bow."

Once they filled their plates, the three of them— Crumpet eyeing the food the entire time—walked over to a table on the outskirts of the small crowd. Roz set her plate down on the table, then tied Crumpet's leash to one of the legs of her chair.

"I've thought about our dinner," Jamie said.

"What did you decide?" To cover her nervousness, Roz feigned intense interest in the food on her plate.

"I called several restaurants, and none of them were interested in having a bulldog as one of their clientele."

"Did you want Crumpet along?"

"Now, I'm not saying that he isn't terrific company. And it would be a quiet evening, because good restaurants generally don't have television sets. But I was thinking of something a little more—romantic."

"I can't ask Jesse to look after him; he'll be performing tomorrow night."

"What I was thinking was maybe we could have dinner right here and Crumpet could join us."

"Right here? At the mansion?"

"Right here on the patio. I'll cook."

"I didn't know you could cook."

"That's because you fell asleep the one time I cooked my omelet."

"We could order out. I think you're on intimate terms with every fast-food establishment in Beverly Hills."

"This has to be different. Trust me."

"So Crumpet and I appear on the terrace at—"

"Seven-thirty for cocktails. Eight for dinner."

She appreciated his joking, for she knew he was deliberately trying to make this easy for her. And he was succeeding. She was looking forward to their evening together. Ever since they had laughed together on the kitchen floor this morning, Roz had felt much more relaxed around him.

This time, nothing was going to go wrong.

HAROLD AND DEENA left amid a flurry of rice and congratulations. But Roz had been sure her mother was going to try to make her point one more time, and she had suspected right.

When Deena and Harold came down the elaborate winding staircase and everyone was standing in the immense hallway, Harold announced it was time for Deena to throw her bouquet. Roz immediately moved to the back of the crowd, Crumpet close at her side. Jamie was talking to Eddie. When Deena raised her arm up, bouquet in hand, the group below was silent for just an instant. Then the bride turned her back, but not before finding her daughter in the crowd.

She tossed the bouquet, and it landed close to Roz on the floor. When Deena turned around, her eyes went directly to her daughter's, and Roz glared at her mother. Then she heard people starting to laugh. Looking down, she saw Crumpet at her feet, the bouquet in his mouth. He had trotted over to sit in front of her, then slowly, unsteadily, he raised up his front paws and begged.

The people around her began to clap, and with a flushed face, Roz knelt down and took the elaborate bouquet out of the bulldog's mouth. As she slowly straightened, she refused to meet her mother's gaze. Instead, her eyes caught Jamie's.

He was smiling.

Chapter Six

Roz was restless the next morning, so after she fed all the animals, she went out to the front yard and helped Tom with some yard work. He had long ago welcomed her presence when she made it clear it in no way threatened his job. She loved to work with her hands, especially with plants. It was the best way to calm down and organize her thoughts.

They were weeding around the flower beds when Jamie came out, a cup of coffee in his hands. He was dressed in a pair of running shorts, a T-shirt and jogging shoes. Roz, in jeans that had seen better days and a crocheted halter top, her hair pulled up on top of her head in a messy bun, shaded her eyes from the sun and glanced up at him.

"You slept in," she remarked.

"Someone turned off my alarm."

"You looked tired yesterday. It's not like my schedule is going to fall apart if you're not out of bed by dawn."

He seemed worried, so she tried to reassure him. "Besides, you and Crumpet looked so cute curled up next to each other."

He smiled. "So that's why I dreamed I was a construction worker. That guy really snores." Crumpet, who had trotted out at Jamie's heels, came over to Roz and gave her face a quick swipe with his tongue.

"Are you hungry, Crumpet?"

The bulldog barked, then began racing around in circles.

"Don't let that mooch fool you. I measured out his food, and he already ate. I was just going to take him on his run."

Roz stood up and wiped her hands off on her jeans. "Why don't I get his Frisbee and we can toss it back and forth. It's kind of hot out, and I don't want him to get overheated."

"Let's go in back."

Roz ran to her Toyota and unlocked it, then pulled a bright yellow Frisbee out of the back seat. The minute Crumpet saw it, he began to bark furiously and run toward her.

"He won't be running around long in this weather; we can just do it right here."

She and Jamie tossed the Frisbee back and forth, Crumpet chasing it furiously. They were careful to stay out of Tom's way. Roz watched Crumpet carefully, but the bulldog showed no signs of heat exhaustion.

"This time let him have it," Jamie called as he threw the Frisbee. Crumpet galloped furiously after it, then caught it and began to shake his head furiously. He pranced over by Roz's Toyota and lay down in a patch of shade. The Frisbee remained between his paws, but when he let go of it, he was panting softly.

"I think that's it for today." Roz felt a piece of hair tickling her neck and reached up into her bun for a hairpin. "You can go ahead and run, Jamie. I'll just stay here with Crumpet and—"

What happened next was so sudden it seemed like a blur. Roz heard an engine revving and turned in time to see a dark sports car come squealing up the driveway directly toward Crumpet. The bulldog cocked his head at the sound of the noise and got to his feet but was clearly too tired to move quickly. A scream rose in her throat, and her legs began to move as she raced toward the dog. She felt Jamie brush past her, his legs pumping incredibly fast, then saw him dive for Crumpet.

He caught the bulldog in the chest, and they both went crashing into the bougainvillea bushes that lined the wide drive. The sports car slammed into the back of Roz's Toyota, metal grinding against metal with a sickening sound.

Roz stopped, her legs trembling. Tom was standing beside her, hedge clippers in his hand. She watched as a man with a black knit ski mask got out of the sports car and, leaving the door open, began to run back down the driveway.

Without thinking, anger bubbling up inside her, she began to race after him.

She was halfway down the drive when the man turned and she saw the gun in his hand. She froze, and automatically her hands went up over her head. The man backed up several paces, the gun still trained on her, then turned and began to run down to the end of the drive. Another car waited there, and she watched as he got in the passenger side and the car squealed away.

She was still shaking when Jamie reached her. He came up behind her and grabbed her around the waist.

"Damn it, Roz, don't you *ever* chase after anyone like that. I don't care what he does! You could have gotten yourself killed!" Then he turned her in his arms at the same time she moved toward him, and he was holding her tightly, his warm arms wrapped securely around her trembling body. It took her a minute before she realized he was shaking, too.

"He had a gun," she whispered hoarsely, then bit her lip to stop from trembling. Funny how when that man had pointed it at her, she had been strangely clearheaded. Now that it was all over and he couldn't possibly hurt her, she was falling apart.

Jamie hugged her tighter. There was something warm on her legs, and when she looked down, she saw he'd scraped his knee badly. There were bits of pebbles in the skin, and blood was running down his shin.

"You're hurt!"

He grimaced. "It could have been a lot worse."

"Here, lean on me. I have a first-aid kit in the kitchen. When they came up the drive, she noticed Tom sitting on the grass, holding Crumpet by his collar. The bulldog was quivering with excitement, and when Roz nodded, Tom let the animal go.

He covered the distance between them in a flash, jumping up on Jamie and swiping at his legs with his tongue.

"He thinks it's a new game," Jamie said through gritted teeth. No matter how brave he acted, Roz knew his leg was hurting badly.

"He's all right, then?"

"Not a scratch. I was trying to untangle us in the bushes so I could go after that guy, but I think Crumpet thought he was supposed to tackle me next."

"Oh, Jamie, I'm so sorry."

"It's okay. Crumpet's okay."

She shut her eyes, her breakfast rising in her throat at the thought of Crumpet being caught between the two cars. The bulldog would have been killed instantly.

Once inside the kitchen, Roz cleaned and bandaged Jamie's leg, gave Crumpet a bone and turned on a game show to keep him amused, then made a pot of coffee. She bit her lip to keep her hands steady as she poured first Jamie, then herself, a cup.

When she sat down next to him, she said the first thing that popped into her head.

"Why would anyone want Crumpet killed?"

Jamie fixed her with a look she'd never seen before. He was all business now; there was none of the man she'd laughed and joked with the morning before.

"Can you think of anyone who would want to kill him?" he asked.

"Any of Matthew's children, from what happened when the will was read. But it wouldn't do them any good. The money still wouldn't go to any of them; Matthew made sure of that."

"Anyone else?"

"He had enemies, Jamie. But I think they would have been glad to see him dead, not interested in killing his dog."

"If you think of anyone, anyone at all, at any time, will you let me know?"

"Why?" Now she was curious. Why was he asking her all these questions? What could Jamie possibly do to help? "Jamie, I appreciate your help, but I think we'd better call the police."

He closed his eyes and put his hand over his forehead. Remembering what Jamie had been through only minutes before, Roz put her hand on his arm. "I can't thank you enough for what you did."

"I love the dog, too, Roz. I would have hated to see him crushed between those cars." He took a long, shuddering sigh. "Those guys, whoever they are, mean business. I don't think they're going to stop until the dog is dead."

As if on cue, Crumpet started barking. On the small television screen, one of the contestants had just spun a giant wheel. It whirled around, then slowed to a stop. The audience roared, and Crumpet barked softly, once, twice, then resumed chewing on the beef bone.

"I'd miss that little guy," Jamie said softly.

Roz felt her eyes beginning to fill with tears. In a delayed reaction, she put her head down on her arms and started to cry.

"Hey, hey, it's all right. Nothing happened. We can get the car fixed, and after we call the police, we can—"

"I don't *care* about the car! Crumpet could have been killed. *You* could have been killed!" She reached for him, her arms going around his neck as she hugged him tightly.

"Roz, I'm all right. They caught us off guard because they didn't do anything for a couple of weeks. Now that we know they're still around, we can fight back. I don't want you worrying. I'm going to call some friends of mine and have them watch the place. The minute anything looks suspicious they'll report to us."

Roz nodded her head wearily. "I think that would be a good idea. Do you want me to call the police?"

"Let me take care of it. Right now I just want you to try and continue through your day." He caught her chin in his hand and raised her eyes to meet his. "If you let them get to you, they've already won. We're still going to have dinner tonight. We're going to go on as if this never happened, except we're both going to be very careful. Okay?"

"Okay."

"Matthew left you in charge because he knew you could do it, Roz. He knew everything would come out all right in the end if you were here."

She felt her eyes starting to fill again. "I couldn't have done anything if you hadn't been there today. I'm not that fast a runner."

"Crumpet wouldn't have been in the driveway if I hadn't thrown the Frisbee that way. Honey, you can drive yourself crazy with that kind of thinking. He's alive. Working together, we've kept him alive." He smiled. "Besides, you've overlooked the most crucial thing of all."

"What?"

"You're the one who hired me."

ROZ SPENT the rest of the morning in bed, Crumpet at the foot of it, watching *The Gang's All Here* with Carmen Miranda and a cast of hundreds. The bulldog was fascinated with the gigantic headdress of fruit, and when Carmen Miranda sang "The Lady

With the Tutti-Frutti Hat,'' he barked and began to dig around in the covers.

Roz stared at the ceiling as she thought furiously, running all her conversations with Matthew through her head, trying to remember if he had ever mentioned anyone in particular she should be wary of. She even thought of what he had told her about his three children. Matt was a pompous ass; Elizabeth, an overindulged and spoiled woman. The only one he had believed had any sense was Sarah, and even she was too much like her mother.

All of them had worshiped money and power.

But why would they kill a dog if there was nothing in it for them? It had to be someone who had hated Matthew, someone who would look upon Crumpet's death as something that would have hurt Matthew, destroyed him.

Suddenly her mind flashed to a scene in the library, after Matthew's will had been read. She had confronted all three of Matthew's children about the night Crumpet had been flung from the Mercedes, and Elizabeth had been the one who hadn't been able to meet her eyes.

Elizabeth. She was a highly unstable woman. She had been the one who had carried on, accusing Roz of sleeping with Matthew. She was the youngest, easily the most spoiled.

And she was the one who was deepest in debt. Sarah had married money; Matt had a flourishing law practice. Elizabeth didn't know how to do anything else except spend money.

And she had that run-in with that guy. Elizabeth was the type of woman who could pick up the only rat at a party. One afternoon when Roz had come over, Matthew had been distraught. He had confided in her, told her they had sent his youngest child to Switzerland, to a drug rehabilitation clinic high up in the Alps. The man she had been involved with had been a dealer, and Elizabeth had experimented with everything, finishing with a very messy and extremely expensive cocaine addiction.

Elizabeth. She picked up the phone by her bed and dialed the number in Jamie's room.

"I THINK WE MAY BE ON to something," Jamie said, sitting crosslegged on the large bed. He had ordered in a large stuffed pizza, and Crumpet was steadily edging toward the warm carton. Carmen Miranda was no match for pepperoni.

"She'd have to be crazy to want to kill Crumpet. It makes absolutely no sense. I can't believe I didn't think of this when that guy gave Crumpet the poisoned chicken."

"You've been through a lot. All these changes couldn't have been easy on you. Don't be so hard on yourself. The important thing is that you remembered this at all."

"She has a problem with shopping, too. There were several times when Matthew had to bail her out because she'd run up incredible sums on her charge cards. She's not responsible at all, very immature. I think this might be her sick way of trying to get back at Matthew."

"I'm going to investigate this. In the meantime, eat that piece of pizza before Crump here decides to swipe it out of your hand."

They talked through lunch, and Roz was satisfied they had figured out who the culprit was. Reassured, she decided to take a nap after Jamie left. Turning the set on low and finding another movie for Crumpet, she stretched out underneath the covers and promptly fell asleep.

WHEN SHE WOKE UP, she felt something at her feet. Sitting up in bed, she saw a large white box with a silver bow on it. There was a tiny card attached. She stole a quick glance at Crumpet, who was watching a *Star Trek* rerun. Then her attention returned to the package and she reached for the card.

I'll be Fred if you'll be Ginger. Crumpet will love it.

She had to laugh. But she stopped laughing when her fingers folded back the white tissue paper and she saw the dress inside.

It was silver lamé, with a beautifully designed bodice and hundreds of tiny pleats in the full-length skirt. The material shimmered as she took it out of the box. Completely stunned, she slowly slid out of bed until she was holding the dress against her. Then she rushed into the bathroom and looked at it in the full-length mirror.

Stunning. She had never thought of herself as a person who could wear a silver lamé dress, but obviously Jamie thought she could. She spun around, watching the pleats in the skirt flare out around her ankles. It was a dress to go dancing in. A dress to make memories in.

He had thought of everything. There were silver shoes in another box, and a full length slip in another. Roz pulled off the T-shirt she had worn to bed and tried on everything. The dress fit her almost perfectly, except it was a little tight at the waist.

So who needs to eat? Aside from that minor flaw, it was perfect. And it wasn't that tight. When she tried on the shoes, the hem looked perfect.

She had never owned anything quite so lovely. It looked as if it had been spun out of silver, the way the material picked up the light.

And I have some control-top panty hose, so there goes the problem around the waist. She had to stop eating so many pizzas with Jamie and start going shopping again and cooking at home. It was all the fast food that had made a few inches creep back on.

She hung the dress on the bathroom door, then glanced at the clock. It was a little after four, and she and Crumpet didn't have to be out on the terrace until seven-thirty. She had plenty of time to make herself gorgeous.

WHEN SHE STEPPED onto the terrace, Roz felt as if she had been transported into another world. Tiny white lights had been strung through all the shrubbery, even through the pots of flowers surrounding the terrace. A bottle of champagne was chilling in an ice bucket standing by one of the patio tables. There were fresh flowers on the table, and candles. The moonlight was reflected off the surface of the pool, making the water look silver and mysterious.

There wasn't a single sound except for Crumpet's panting. He was standing next to her, a red bow tied jauntily around his neck.

As she glanced around for Jamie, Roz suddenly felt nervous. What was she supposed to do? Did he want her to go sit at the table? Maybe she should go into the kitchen and see if he was there. She was exactly on time, even though she had given herself a manicure, a pedicure, conditioned her hair, set it, then twisted it up. She'd taken great pains with her makeup, removing her eyeliner twice when it wasn't as subtle as she thought it should be. Her eyes looked huge in her face, and her cheekbones were clearly defined by a peachy blusher.

"Come on, Crumpet." She couldn't stand waiting by the French doors forever, so she walked out onto the patio and enjoyed the feel of the silver dress swishing around her legs.

She was standing on the steps leading down to the second level of the terrace when she heard him. Swinging around, she saw a Jamie she had never seen before. Dressed in a black tuxedo, he was carrying two filled champagne flutes. When he saw her, he stopped. She couldn't quite see the expression in his eyes, but the fact that he stopped and stared made her glad she had gone to all the trouble to be beautiful for him.

"Crumpet, stay," she whispered as she started to walk toward him. He met her halfway, and they stood staring at each other. She was at a complete loss for words, and he was looking at her as if he'd never seen her before.

When he finally spoke, he chose the perfect words to put her at ease.

"Hi, Ginger."

She smiled. "Hi, Fred."

Crumpet barked sharply, and remembering she had left him sitting by the steps, Roz snapped her fingers. He came bounding toward them, barking excitedly.

Jamie handed her one of the flutes in his hands, and she took it. He touched her arm briefly, then touched his glass to hers.

"To tonight. To the beginning of you and me."

Crumpet barked again.

"And Crumpet," Jamie added, smiling.

Roz raised her glass to her lips and took a sip of the champagne. The bubbles raced through her mouth, and she tilted her head back slightly and looked up into the sky. It was as dark a sky as you could ever find in Los Angeles, but it was still romantic.

"This is wonderful."

"You've only seen the beginning. Please, would you and Crumpet come this way."

He escorted them to a table set for three. Roz started to laugh as he pulled out a chair and patted the seat. Crumpet struggled into it, but Jamie gave him some assistance. When the bulldog put one chubby white paw on the tabletop, Roz hissed a quiet reprimand.

"Crumpet, no! You sit."

Jamie gave her a confident grin, then reached into his suit pocket. "I thought of every last detail." He pulled out the tiniest television set Roz had ever seen; it had a two-inch screen. He fiddled with it for a few seconds, then set it down on the table so Crumpet could see it. The sound was on very low, and the bulldog stared, fascinated.

"The next time I take him to the vet, I'll take that little TV along. Where did you get it?"

"No questions tonight. You're simply here to enjoy."

It was a simple meal composed of some of her favorite foods. As she ate, she remembered all the casual questions he had asked her during his first weeks at the mansion, and she realized he had been storing information away, remembering. His memory had to be incredible.

First tiger prawns in cocktail sauce. Crumpet scorned seafood and continued to stare at the tiny screen. Then a salad with the lightest vinaigrette. Prime rib, medium rare, with Yorkshire pudding and creamed spinach. Then, for dessert, the most incredible trifle she had ever tasted.

Crumpet was absolutely astounded when his prime rib was set down on the floor by his chair. Even though it was in his bowl, he still looked at Roz before he ate it. When she tapped the side of his bowl lightly, he attacked it.

"You've trained him well."

"He only eats what you and I give him. I've seen him slip up sometimes when Maria gives him leftovers."

"But he's a changed dog. You've accomplished quite a bit with him."

"Speaking of accomplishments, you didn't cook this meal, did you?"

"My heart was in the right place, but by the time I finished at the police station, it was too late to do anything but bribe Lawry's into delivering. But the tiger prawns were my idea; I bought them yesterday at Phil's. With a bottle of their cocktail sauce.''

"So the only thing you really did was mix the sauce in with the shrimp."

"I cannot tell a lie. It was take-out as usual."

"It was wonderful. Jamie, I can't believe this; it's like something out of a dream."

"It's no dream." He was leaning back in his chair, watching her.

"It's been absolutely perfect. The dress, the champagne, Crumpet's TV, the meal . . ."

"And the best is yet to come." He stood up, then helped her ease her chair away from the table. "Let's leave Crumpet to the *Love Boat* and sail away to the lower terrace."

"Jamie—"

"No questions, Roz. Just enjoy."

He took her hand, and she followed him down the steps to the second level of the terrace. It was filled with plants and the greenery was entwined with more sparkling white lights. Roz felt her throat tighten briefly as she remembered the hours she had spent with Matthew, helping him landscape this area. It had been so barren before she had suggested the addition of plants. In the end, the terrace above the pool resembled a lush jungle. Now it seemed as if the plants were all surreal, the white lights twinkling and giving off the softest of glows.

"Stay right here," Jamie said, walking quickly over to the side of the terrace. He was bent over something; she couldn't quite make out what it was. He came back to her side and put one arm around her waist, then took her other hand in his.

"We're just about ready."

A terrible suspicion was beginning to build in Roz's mind. During the dinner, she had been at ease with Jamie, but now she was certain she was going to make a total fool of herself and expose her lack of social expertise.

When the music came on, she was certain. It was one of her favorite tunes, Linda Ronstadt singing classics with Nelson Riddle's orchestra providing the music. But she was so embarrassingly aware of her body's lack of knowledge she could only stare at the cement.

"Roz?" Now he sounded uncertain. "I thought after dinner, we'd go dancing."

She swallowed, once more miserably aware of the gulf between them. So many things Jamie happily took for granted were major boundaries for her to cross.

"I can't dance," she whispered.

"What?"

He hadn't heard her. Standing on tiptoe, she leaned against his chest and whispered in his ear. "Jamie, I can't dance."

He was silent for a moment, and Roz wanted to sink beneath the concrete, or at least go jump in the pool. Anything to get out of this embarrassing moment.

"Do you want to try?" He sounded encouraging.

"Are you a good dancer?"

"I can make my way around the floor. I'm competent."

"I'll step on your feet."

"The only people who are going to see you are me and Crumpet. *I* won't say anything, and he can't."

She smiled then and felt him gently squeeze her hand. "I taught both my little sisters. I've had practice at this."

"You're sure you don't mind?"

He was smiling down at her now, with the tenderest expression in his eyes. "You seem to forget what's in it for me. I get to hold you in my arms."

"Don't get mad at me if I'm not good at this right away."

He kissed the tip of her nose, and she felt her stomach flip-flop crazily. "I give you my official permission to be absolutely awful. We can fall all over the cement, be out of step. There's only one absolute requirement."

"What's that?" She was sure she'd be incapable of doing it.

"You have to have fun. The minute this evening stops being fun for you, we stop."

It's not fun right now. She didn't want Jamie to think of her as a clumsy incompetent, as someone who had none of the basic social skills. At the same time, however, she knew he had gone to so much trouble to set everything up. He had wanted to treat her to an evening of dancing underneath the stars.

She couldn't let him down.

"I almost lost you there, didn't I."

"I'm ready."

His hand tightened on her waist. "I'm going to go real slow. Just watch what I do and kind of follow my lead. And listen to Linda."

He was as good as his word, moving slowly, whispering easy directions in her ear. At first, her body seemed stiff and foreign. She felt as vulnerable as a baby taking its first steps. But somewhere in the middle of the fifth song her feet began moving of their own accord, and she managed to look up and smile into Jamie's face.

"There you go! Stop thinking and let it happen. Roz, you're wonderful at this."

She smiled then and pressed her cheek against his chest. Closing her eyes, she felt the exact moment when her body seemed to become a part of his. Their steps were in rhythm, each one attuned to the other's movement. In his arms she felt safe and secure and loved. And beautiful.

Another song finished, and they stood still, waiting for the next. As the first notes floated out over the still night air, she stepped slightly away from Jamie and looked up at his face.

"This is one of my favorites."

"Mine, too. It reminds me of you." As they gazed into each other's eyes, Linda began to sing the first lyrics of "Someone to Watch Over Me." Her voice was emotional, haunting, filled with romantic melancholy.

"We have an audience," Jamie whispered as he took his first step.

She followed him but twisted her head around, wondering who could be watching them. What she saw made her grin. Crumpet had abandoned his television and was sitting in his chair, his broad face split into a doggy grin, his tongue lolling out of his mouth. He seemed fascinated with the two of them and was watching their every move.

"He probably has us confused with a Busby Berkeley movie," Jamie whispered.

"I don't think so."

"Why would he be staring at us that way unless we looked like something on TV?"

"He likes the skirt of my dress. Maybe that's it."

"I like that dress, too. I like what's inside it better. Did I tell you you look beautiful tonight?"

"As many times as I told you."

He kissed her cheek. "I'll tell you again. Roz, you're a knockout. I don't want you going to the supermarket in that dress."

She laughed and missed a step. Crumpet barked, and his body began to wiggle as he wagged his stumpy tail.

"He's a tough taskmaster, Roz. If you miss a step, it upsets him."

"Then I won't."

And she didn't. With practice came confidence, and she followed Jamie as he began to move freely around the stone terrace, his movements becoming more sweeping and daring.

"Competent, huh?"

"Hey, I got a lot of practice teaching my sisters."

"You're really good."

"I had two tough students."

"Three."

He laughed then and gathered her closer into his arms as he swept her around and around the terrace. Crumpet was barking furiously now, and out of the corner of her mind she heard his chair scrape as he jumped down, then his panting as he ran down the stairs. He began to race around the two of them, jumping and barking.

"I think this is his favorite game of all," Jamie said.

Roz couldn't think. She felt as if she were whirling faster, closer to something she'd wanted from the time she was a little girl. Jamie slowed his steps. She followed him, and when they stopped, they were standing close to each other.

She couldn't stop looking at his face. He was the same Jamie she had started the evening with, but something was different. *She* was different. Everything about his face was so special. Her heart was thundering inside her chest, and she knew it wasn't from dancing.

"Jamie?" Her voice trembled slightly. *What's happening to me?* Within seconds after she asked herself the question, she knew.

She wanted to remember everything about this exact moment forever, but the bright lights at the side of her vision were blurring. Everything was blurring, colors and sounds washing together as she watched his face coming closer to hers.

She reacted from pure instinct, listening to her heart's wishes. Closing her eyes, she tilted her head slightly, then felt his lips covering hers.

This time there was no holding back, no fear. Her body, still loose and warm from dancing, melted into his as his arms came firmly around her waist. She gave in to an impulse she didn't even know she had until she acted on it and touched his hair with her fingers, then buried them in the slightly longer hair brushing his tuxedo jacket.

It was a different kiss from the one in the kitchen. That had been a first kiss—tentative, gentle. But as she responded now, she felt him beginning to lead her into a deeper intimacy.

When he broke the contact, he kissed her again. And again. Soft kisses, one after the other. She surprised herself, kissing him back, running her hands over his shoulders and back up into his hair. He was pressing her tightly against his body, and it felt so very right, the softness of hers against the hardness of his. It was as if they were dancing again, each following the other, whirling closer and closer to something Roz now knew she wanted.

IT WAS WARM in Jamie's bedroom, but even so Roz shivered when he unzipped the back of her silver dress. He was kissing her back, and she closed her eyes as sensations she had never experienced before raced through her body.

The dress slid to the floor, a pool of spun silver at her feet. Turning slowly, suddenly shy with him, she kept her eyes on the floor for just an instant before looking up at his face.

The same warmth was there, the same caring, but there was also something purely masculine in the way his gaze slid quickly over her body. It was as if he were touching each place he looked at. She had never realized simply looking at someone could be so exciting.

He had taken off his jacket and slung it over the chair by his bed. Wanting to touch him and sensing he was going to wait for her to make the next move, she stepped out of the dress and laid her palms against his chest. His skin was hot, even through the shirt, and her fingers moved to the buttons. She wanted to touch his skin, to feel it against hers. In the past, when she had thought about moments like this, she had been frightened. Now, with Jamie, she felt a sense of inevitability washing over her like the tide. Not only could she not stop what was about to happen; she wanted it to.

He stood perfectly still as she unbuttoned his shirt, but when she pushed it apart and over his shoulders, her palms running over the hair on his chest, she felt his muscles tighten and a peculiar little shudder run through his body. It emboldened her, and she gently pulled the shirt out of his waistband, then eased it off his arms and let it drop to the floor.

He kissed her again—her cheeks, her mouth, then her neck. Her breath came out in a short, sharp gasp as she felt him press his lips against the cleft between her breasts.

"Beautiful." The word was whispered, but there was a rough emotional quality to his voice.

She felt him easing her down on his bed, and then they were lying across it, she in her silk slip, he in his tuxedo pants. He moved his body so he was slightly above her, though not on top of her, and looked down at her. The lamp by his bed was turned to its lowest setting, so she could see the expression on his face.

Even in passion he thought of her.

"You're sure?" he asked quietly.

She nodded her head. *Tell him now.* But she didn't quite know how to say it.

She felt Jamie's hand move up from her waist, then cup one of her breasts. His hand outside the silk felt exquisitely pleasurable, but she wanted to be closer to him, feel his hands against her naked skin. She reached up and slid the strap of her slip down her upper arm. He kissed her shoulder; then she felt his finger hook underneath the lace and pull it farther down. She shuddered as she felt his lips against her breast.

The time for words was long past. She lay very still as he eased the top of her slip down around her waist. Naked from the waist up, she felt vulnerable beneath his gaze.

But the minute he touched her breast, she closed her eyes and gave herself up to feeling. He was gentle with her, his fingers light and sure, and she reached up and held him, wanting this closeness and everything that followed.

When his lips moved to her breast, she arched beneath him, offering him everything she had to give, body, soul and heart. His touch was slightly less gentle now, more urgent and demanding. She felt she was on the brink of understanding so much when the sound of her deep breathing and short little sighs was broken by a snore.

Jamie raised his head up, a look of utter confusion on his face as he stared down at her. Roz lay perfectly still, wondering where the noise had come from.

They heard it again and glanced over at the television. Crumpet was stretched out in front of it, his head resting against his paws. Snoring. The moment was broken.

"I forgot about Crumpet," Roz admitted.

"He must have been busy with our leftovers when I carried you upstairs."

"Do you mind him being here?" she asked.

"I figure it's the same as your dancing. Who's he going to tell?"

She smiled, then lay back down on the bed. He followed her and kissed her with a thoroughness that left her feeling soft and pliant.

"Besides," Jamie whispered. "Who'd believe him?"

Sighing, Jamie lay his head back down between her breasts. Her hands went to his hair, smoothing it with a comforting motion.

"I never thought I would spend time with you in bed and wonder where the *TV Guide* was." His voice was slightly muffled against her skin.

She smiled, her lips still tender. "It's on top of the television."

Slowly, his whole posture one of almost total defeat, Jamie got up off the bed, then brought the magazine back. He propped some pillows against his headboard, then lay back and motioned for Roz to join him.

She lay against his chest, and they both studied the guide.

"There's a Disney movie at midnight on cable."

"It's *101 Dalmations*. We'd be up all night."

"Does he bark at cartoon dogs?"

"He barks at cartoons period. I never let him watch most of them; they're getting too violent. Besides, the animation is usually bad."

"Here we are. *The Thin Man*. I know Crumpet likes old movies."

"You forgot Asta."

"Damn it."

"Here's one. *The River*. That was a good film."

"He barks at livestock."

"Let's not get frantic, Roz. Matthew subscribed to every cable channel known to man. There has to be something Crumpet will watch."

One by one they negated all the movies that evening. Finally Jamie put the guide down in disgust.

"Where's Busby Berkeley when you need him? Thank God he didn't use dogs in his films."

"Wait, I thought I saw something—" She reached for the guide and flipped it back open. "I wonder if Crumpet would sit still for this." She pointed to one of the columns.

"The French Chef?"

"Why not? It's about food."

"It's also thirty minutes long."

She flipped the guide closed. "We could always put him in my bedroom." She knew she sounded tentative.

"No. He's used to sleeping with one of us. We just have to find a good movie sometime soon."

"Thank you, Jamie." She slid her arms around his waist and hugged him tightly. "I'd never forgive myself if something happened to him. Until this whole mess is cleared up, I feel safer if Crumpet is somewhere I can see him. Or with you."

He started to grin. "That definitely limits our possibilities."

They were silent for a moment, then Jamie picked up the guide. *"The French Chef,* huh?"

"It might work."

He tuned in the television with the remote control, then quickly flipped to the channel. Julia Child was bustling through her kitchen.

"And once you have the chicken, you brown it slowly..."

The snores stopped. Crumpet slowly raised his head, his ears perked toward the screen.

"Then you pour in the wine..."

He snorted, then inched closer to the screen.

Jamie turned off the light by the bed so that the room was illuminated by the television. Crumpet's head blocked almost the entire screen, he was so close. The only sound in the bedroom was that of chicken being fried.

"Now I call this romantic." Jamie enfolded her in his arms and lay back down on the bed, tossing the pillow aside. "Thirty minutes?"

"Twenty-five."

"I think we're going to have to settle for a few kisses and a glass of champagne."

SHE SPENT THE NIGHT in his bed, Crumpet sleeping soundly at the foot. During the night, Roz woke up once. She was lying on her side, Jamie behind her. His arms were around her, one on her hip, the other on her breast. She was glad they had fallen asleep together; she hadn't wanted the feeling of closeness to end. Sleeping with Jamie was strange. She had never slept in the same bed with anyone before. She could hear his heartbeat; it matched her own. He breathed deeply, and she felt his fingers tighten on her hip.

Smiling, she put her hand over his and drifted off to sleep.

JAMIE FELT HIS FACE being tickled. Deep in the recesses of his mind, he knew Roz wasn't likely to wake him up by running her tongue over his face. They were barely past kissing.

He opened his eyes and stared into Crumpet's. When the bulldog realized he was awake, he began to wag his stubby tail.

"I know, I know," Jamie grumbled, sitting up in the rumpled sheets. "So many meals, so little time. C'mere boy."

Crumpet shot into his arms as Jamie picked up the *TV Guide.*

"Now there's got to be something here that can occupy you for an evening. I don't want you to think Roz and I don't want you around, but we don't want you around."

Crumpet butted his head against Jamie's free hand, and he automatically began to scratch the dog's head. He scanned the guide, especially the movie channels. When he finally saw what he was looking for, it was so close to what he hoped he'd find he couldn't believe his luck.

"God bless Channel Nine."

A Busby Berkeley festival. *Gold Diggers of 1935,* followed by *I Live For Love, Bright Lights, Stage Struck, Strike Up the Band, Babes on Broadway* and ending with *For Me and My Gal.*

"Crumpet," he said softly as he began to mark the days and times, "I think you and I are both in for the best time of our lives."

WHERE ARE YOU GOING?"

"Crumpet and I are going down to Crown Books. They have a sale on videotapes."

"What are you going to record?"

"It's a surprise."

THAT EVENING, as they were sitting at the kitchen table and eating cheese enchiladas, Roz tried to put her feelings into words.

"Jamie, about last night—I think we—I need to talk."

His blue eyes were anxious as he looked at her, and she was surprised to realize he was nervous, too.

"I don't mean—I mean, I usually don't—"

"I know."

"You do?"

He covered her hand with his, and she felt his fingers, warm and strong, against her own. "Roz, if it makes any difference to you, I want you to know that I don't go in for casual—affairs. I don't even like the word."

"But you seem—I mean, I bet a lot of women would be attracted to you." There. It was out. All through the morning she had wondered, *why me?* when Jamie could obviously have anyone he wanted.

"But that has nothing to do with us. I could say the same thing. A lot of men could be attracted to you."

There was a short silence while she tried to digest this but couldn't. Try as she might, Roz couldn't quite see herself as being attractive to the opposite sex. It was different with Jamie, because he was different from any other man she had ever met.

She tried again. "I think part of it was because things were so romantic last night. It kind of swept me away with the moment."

"Are you regretting it this morning?" Now the familiar intense expression was back in his eyes, and she knew her answer was important to him.

"No." She lowered her eyes to the table. "I've watched you for a long time and wondered what it would be like to..." She let her voice trail off, then glanced up at his face. There was a smile in his eyes as his lips started to curve upward.

"That makes me feel great." He squeezed her hand. "I've been watching you, too."

"You have?"

"Yeah."

"Oh."

"I think we have only one problem, Roz."

She could feel herself tensing. "What's that?" *It has to be something I did.*

"Bulldog interruptus."

She saw the mischievous gleam in his eyes and bit her lip against her laughter.

"This sounds serious. What should we do?" The words were out of her mouth before she thought them through, and she was delighted that she could tease him back and be witty and wonderful, like the people she'd grown up with on television.

"We'll have to be very clever in order to rid ourselves of this problem. Of course, we don't want the bulldog in question to feel slighted."

"Of course not."

"And we don't want to leave him alone for too long. There's no telling what kind of trouble he could get into."

"What's left?"

He lifted her fingers to his lips and gave her hand a quick kiss. "We have ways. I'm working on it as we speak."

"You are?"

"No hints. I want it to be a surprise."

"Give me one hint—"

She was interrupted by a desperate, anguished squeal. The sound made Roz's stomach tighten and her hands clench.

"Champ! Oh, my God—"

An instant after the squeal they both heard vicious snarls. Crumpet shot out from underneath the table and disappeared down the hall toward the front of the mansion.

Within seconds, Jamie had followed. Roz raced behind him, silently praying the entire time they wouldn't be too late.

When they reached the library where the snarls were coming from, she was shocked to see Kai attacking a man dressed entirely in black, a ski mask over his head. The husky had the intruder's gun hand in her mouth and was shaking her head back and forth, snarling guttural growls from deep in her throat.

Champ was cowering behind the sofa, and when he attempted to run toward Roz, she noticed his left hind leg was hurt.

"Kai!"

The husky let go of the man's arm, and he began to run toward the window.

"Freeze!" Jamie had picked up the man's gun from where he'd dropped it on the Oriental rug and now had it trained on the intruder. He kept running.

Raising the gun above his head, Jamie fired.

The noise was deafening, and Roz flinched at the sound. But the intruder froze, and she watched, horrified, as Jamie ran toward him.

"Roz, give me your belt. Cover me."

Her fingers numb, she obeyed him, the gun cold in her hands, then watched as he used the rope belt to securely tie the man's hands behind his back. Taking back the gun, Jamie nudged its muzzle against the intruder's shoulder blades.

"Now *move*."

Roz couldn't keep the sick feeling from invading her stomach. He was a stranger to her, this Jamie. There was too much expertise in the way he had handled the gun, in the authority in his voice. He was a quick thinker, but no one was that expert in an emergency of this sort unless he'd had plenty of practice.

He was no butler.

Back in the kitchen, she found Jamie some rope, and he tied the burglar in one of the heavy wooden chairs. Only then did he jerk the man's ski mask over his head.

He was an ugly fellow, not so much from the combination of features as from the expression in his eyes and around his mouth. This man was violent. Dangerous.

Keeping the gun trained on him, Jamie said softly, "Roz, I want you to call the police. Ask for Officer Jenner. Tell him we have someone who'd like to spend some time with him."

She reached for the kitchen phone, but his voice, still soft and reassuring, stopped her.

"Take the dogs upstairs to your bedroom. You don't want to be down here when I ask this man what he was doing here tonight."

She didn't even think of disobeying him.

Upstairs in her room, she lay Champ on the bed and examined him. The bulldog was whimpering, and his leg was sticking out at an odd angle. After she called the police, she called Dr. Ramsey.

She stayed upstairs the entire time, except when she showed Officer Jennings and Dr. Ramsey in the front door. The vet checked Champ over and confirmed her suspicions.

The leg was broken.

"It looks like he grabbed the animal by his leg and picked him up. There's no doubt about it, Rosalind; he meant to harm him. Probably would have killed him if that husky of yours hadn't attacked."

She reached down and ran her fingers through the silky hair on Kai's head. Crumpet was pressed close to her other side. She had locked Sheba and Sting in Jamie's bedroom, and Rocky was still in hiding in her bathroom, but the animals were picking up the tension inside the mansion. She could hear the shepherd and the Labrador beginning to bark.

"Can you set it here? Champ goes crazy when he's in the kennel." The dog, though he had come a long way, was still frightened of anyone but Rosalind. He had been as bad as Rocky when she'd found him.

"You set up that little room in the stable, didn't you?"

She nodded.

"I'll do it there, then. I want you to carry him down and sit with him; otherwise, he'll be too frightened."

As she and Dr. Ramsey were walking down the stairs, she saw the intruder, handcuffed, being led out the door by two police officers. Jamie was standing by Jennings, and the police officer was listening intently.

"He had to be after Crumpet. The dogs are similar in breed and coloring. This is the second time this week . . ."

Her mind and body numb, she followed the vet out to the stable.

Later in the evening, once Champ was settled in her bathroom with Rocky, and Kai had been given a bone, Roz sat on the chair by her bed. Crumpet's head rested on her feet.

It was only a matter of time. After the poisoned chicken, she had thought whoever it was had given up. But within days, Crumpet's life had been threatened twice. First, the man in the sports car. Now the intruder tonight.

It was completely foreign to her, the idea of killing an animal, no matter what could be gained. There were some that had to be destroyed, mostly because of disease or intense pain. Some animals had temperament problems, and though she worked with them as much as possible, they would never improve.

She had seen her fair share of animals put to sleep, but she couldn't understand why anyone would want to harm Crumpet.

"Matthew should have just given you to me, Crumpet. He never should have involved us with the money." She had never doubted her friend's judgment before tonight. But now she was scared. If things kept up like this, if Crumpet's life was continually under assault, would they win in the end?

She felt his presence and looked up to see Jamie standing in her doorway. She stared at him, studying him as if she had just met him. And it was true, for tonight she had come face-to-face with another side of his personality, and she suddenly felt that the smiling, patient, fun-loving Jamie had been a cover-up for the man she had seen in action tonight.

That man had been utterly ruthless, violent and dangerous. There had been a coldness in his face as he'd tied the burglar's hands, an intensity to his entire body when he'd picked up the gun.

He wasn't the Jamie she knew. Or loved.

When she finally spoke the words, they came out flat and cold. Almost dead.

"Who are you, really?"

Chapter Seven

Murdered. Matthew had been murdered. Roz closed her eyes and pulled the covers up around her shoulders. There was one thing in Jamie's favor, once she had asked him to tell her the truth. He hadn't lied. He had sat down on the edge of her bed, facing her chair, and quietly told her everything.

His mother and Matthew had been friends for years. Meryl had suspected murder, and once the coroner had confirmed it, she had asked her second son to infiltrate the household, use his skills as a private investigator, and figure out who could have killed Matthew. And why.

He had even told her she'd been the chief suspect for a very short time. "But not now," he'd added quickly.

"What made you change your mind?" She had been emotionally destroyed by his having lied to her, even if at first he had had to—and later he had wanted to protect her. Her darker thoughts she kept to the back of her consciousness, not wanting to face them yet.

"It didn't add up. A woman who takes animals and nurses them back to life wouldn't commit murder. I trust my instincts, and they were screaming at me that you couldn't have murdered Matthew."

She couldn't stop the next question from bubbling out, although she wasn't sure she wanted to hear the answer.

"Was the—was the dinner and the dancing and everything—I mean, were you still collecting information for—"

"No, Roz. That had nothing to do with any of this and everything to do with you and me."

"I feel like I don't know you. I feel like I've shown you all there is of me and there's still so much I don't know about you. When you had that gun in your hand, it was as if you were a different person."

"That's my work. Roz, what you've seen here in this mansion, that's me. That's the real Jamie."

"But do you understand how I'd be scared? How I'd feel I didn't know anything about you or who you really are?"

He'd sighed then and looked her straight in the eye. "I was going to tell you. I'd been thinking about it for a long time. I knew I could trust you, knew you had nothing to do with the murder. But there was so much that had changed in your life. In the beginning, I couldn't tell you. Later, I thought the case would be solved and I could tell you afterward."

"And now?"

"Now I'm moving into the adjoining bedroom. I'll be carrying a gun with me at all times. I don't want either you or Crumpet out of my sight. We have to face the obvious."

"And what's that?"

"They may come after you. You know too much. In order to dispose of Crumpet, they may try to get you, too."

Wrapped in a blanket and lying in bed, Roz felt more confined than ever. If the mansion had seemed like a prison before, now she was truly trapped.

"But what do we do?" she had asked him. "Wait for them to come after us again?"

"That's exactly what we have to do. That, and dig up every bit of information we can on the Barretts. That's one good thing about this. Now you know where I've been spending my time out of the house, and you can help me."

"I'll help you in any way I can. Matthew once gave me a list of his close friends in case I ever needed help and he wasn't available. I could give that list to you, and you could ask them questions."

"That's a terrific lead."

"I don't know how to do research that well, but if you tell me what to do, I can help you."

"You'll do just fine. But what I want you to do right now is try and get some sleep. We've got some rough times ahead of us."

Her throat was tight. "I keep thinking about Matthew. I can't understand how anyone could kill him."

"I don't, either. But someone did. Now try and sleep. Just lie down and close your eyes, okay? I'll be nearby."

She tried to sleep, but her feelings were in turmoil. Even if she and Crumpet did get out of this nightmare alive, would it be possible to have a relationship with a man who was constantly in danger? She didn't believe Jamie was lying to her about his feelings. What he said to her felt right, and she didn't believe it was her own wishful thinking. Working with animals for so many years, she'd had to become adept at nonverbal communication. Everything she noticed about Jamie, the way he was with her, added up to a man who cared.

Can we do it? Roz had never been a blindly optimistic person. Since she'd been small, she had noticed life didn't always reward people even if they were good. There was evil in the world, as well, and many times it triumphed. Though she believed that ultimately there had to be a karmic law that evened things up, she knew it didn't necessarily have to happen in this lifetime.

"C'mere, Crumpet," she called softly.

The bulldog jumped on the bed and walked up to her face, then lay down and sighed. She looked into the mournful dark eyes and wondered if she and Crumpet would survive the nightmare that lay ahead.

JAMIE LAY BACK on the king-size bed in the adjoining bedroom. *Better it's all out in the open.* He heard Roz call Crumpet, then the squeak of the mattress as the dog jumped up. More than anything, he wished he could go in and comfort her, but he knew she needed time by herself to assimilate what had just happened.

It was a lot to take in for one day. He was a private investigator. Matthew had been murdered. Her own life was in danger. He wasn't really sure if they would try for Rosalind, but as long as she knew who he was, he wanted to keep her as close as possible.

It was nothing he could put his finger on, just a feeling. The killer was not acting in a logical way. The attempts on Crumpet's life had been sloppy, badly timed. They were dealing with an amateur, but that didn't make the murderer any less dangerous. Amateurs panicked, and then the results were disastrous for everyone.

The latest intruder was refusing to talk, even though the police had been questioning him relentlessly. Jamie had been hoping the man would slip and tell them who had hired him. But he was closemouthed, and they were getting nowhere. It was frustrating to be so close, yet so far away from the answer.

The attacks were coming closer and closer together. The killer was getting impatient. Desperate. If they could just wait a little longer, they might be able to smoke him out.

The alarm by his bed buzzed softly, and he clicked it off. What had he been meaning to do at eleven? He searched his mind, then remembered.

Gold Diggers of 1935.

He wouldn't disturb Crumpet now. He'd leave the dog with Roz. Getting up as quietly as he could, he headed in the direction of his old bedroom.

STILL UNABLE TO SLEEP, Roz needed an escape more than ever. She flipped through the channels until she found what she wanted, a light, romantic comedy. But it was strangely unsatisfying, and she watched it with unseeing eyes.

Would Jamie be with you now if none of this had happened?

More than anything, she had wanted to ask him to watch the movie with her, but she couldn't. She still needed some distance, time to put things in perspective.

When the phone rang, she was startled. Before she answered it, Jamie appeared at the door adjoining their bedrooms, his phone in hand.

"Pick it up when I do," he said softly.

She did as he instructed.

"Hello?" Her voice sounded calm, but she certainly wasn't. Nothing seemed safe to her now, not even the telephone.

"Is this Rosalind?"

"Yes, it is." Out of the corner of her eye, she caught sight of Jamie. He nodded his head slightly, and she knew he was pleased she hadn't panicked and hung up the phone.

"This is Elizabeth. I was wondering if you would be available to meet with me and my brother tomorrow. We'd like to make you an offer."

There was nothing she wanted to do less. But she looked up at Jamie. There was a tense expression on his face, a tightness around his mouth, but he slowly nodded his head.

"Yes, I think that could be arranged. Where would you like to meet and what time?"

"My lawyer's office is in Beverly Hills. Mr. Rissman on Camden. I was thinking around three, if that would be convenient."

"That would be fine."

"I'll see you tomorrow. Oh, and Rosalind?"

"Yes."

"Think very carefully about this meeting tomorrow. We're prepared to give you a generous offer, and I think you would be wise to take it."

"Good night, Elizabeth."

When she hung up the phone, Jamie did the same. He walked to the bed and sat down, then reached over and began to ruffle Crumpet's ears.

"I'm going with you. So is Crumpet. They might try something while you're out of the house. I want you to watch their reactions to the dog. I think we may be able to find out a great deal that could help us."

"What if they try to hurt him?"

"They won't expect you to bring him. We'll leave Kai loose in the mansion and take extra precautions. I'm going to ask one of the men to stand guard by your bathroom so they can't get to Champ or Rocky."

"Jamie, I'm scared."

"We're dealing with people who aren't very bright, and sometimes they can be the worst. I don't think it's going to be long now."

"Jamie, would you—"

"Anything."

"Oh, God, this is difficult to say. Would you sleep in bed with Crumpet and me? I mean, not to do anything, but just so I could feel safe."

He put his arm around her shoulders and squeezed gently. "I wanted to suggest it, but I didn't know how you'd feel. I'd be glad to."

IT TOOK ROZ A LONG TIME to fall asleep that night.

"Restless?" Jamie asked softly.

"I just keep waiting to hear a noise. I feel like something's going to happen." Jamie seemed like a total stranger to her now.

He was sitting up in bed. His shoulder holster looked menacing against his T-shirt. Roz could feel the tension in his body. He was alert and watchful. She felt perfectly safe with him, but she just couldn't relax enough to go to sleep.

Crumpet was curled up on the foot of the bed, snoring.

"Would you mind if I smoked?" he asked softly.

"I didn't know you smoked."

"Only when I'm nervous."

"It's okay."

He sighed, and she watched as he pulled a blue packet of cigarettes out of the jacket he'd slung over a nearby chair.

"We're dealing with a pretty strange person, Roz. Three different times he's tried to kill Crumpet, and he wasn't fooling around. Poisoning the chicken, then trying to run him over, then breaking Champ's leg. If this person ever gets Crumpet, it'll be all over."

"How long do you think it'll be before we catch him?"

"Soon. There's a desperate, uneven rhythm to his attempts. He's trying to scare us. This meeting tomorrow—I think everything's coming to a head. That's why I want you to be extra careful."

"I will be. But I wish it would just *end*. How long can we stay cooped up in here? I felt like my life was taken away from me the day I walked into this mansion, and I've never shaken that feeling. I wish it was only the press that was after me. I think I could handle them now."

"Roz, tomorrow, go along with them. Whatever they ask you to do, I want you to act as if you're considering it. Let's put them off their guard."

"So you don't think it's one of Matthew's business enemies?"

"I think it's closer to home. Otherwise, how could he have been poisoned so slowly? It has to be one of his children. From everything both you and my mother have told me, I'm placing my bets on Elizabeth. I think she's the one who needs the money. The other day I found out she's seriously in debt, and neither Matt nor Sarah would give her a loan. Then, bingo, we have two attempts on Crumpet's life after weeks of nothing."

"What if she tries—"

"She won't in a lawyer's office. Besides, I'll have my gun. Nothing is going to happen to you or Crumpet."

Remembering the way he'd handled the burglar in the library, Roz knew he was right.

He lit the cigarette, and the planes of his face were highlighted for just an instant by the flare of the match. He looked different to her now. More menacing.

"Jamie, I want you to know how much I appreciate your help. I was thinking while I was lying in here with Crumpet this afternoon, and I know—neither of us would have a chance if you weren't here."

He exhaled the smoke, tilting his head away from her and holding the cigarette away from the bed.

"I loved him, too, Roz."

IN THE EARLY HOURS before dawn the sound of shattering glass woke Roz. Her heart pounding sicken

ingly, she leaped out of bed, Crumpet at her side.
Jamie was already halfway down the hall.

"Stay back!" His voice floated down the long, dark
hallway. She waited, holding Crumpet's collar, until
she heard him call out it was safe. He was standing in
the doorway of the front living room, and she noticed
immediately there was broken glass all over the Au-
busson carpet.

"A message from our friends. The front window's
broken."

Jesse appeared in the doorway. "What the hell was
that crash?"

"The same people who paid us a visit in the sports
car and later in the library," Roz said.

He glanced at the carpet. "I'll get the broom."

Later, after the glass was cleaned up and Jesse had
returned to his bedroom, Jamie spread the crumpled
note out on the desk in Roz's bedroom. The piece of
paper had been tightly wrapped around the rock that
had broken the window.

Give up the dog.

"It doesn't make any sense! Why would anyone
want Crumpet? Even if they thought it would hurt
Matthew, he's dead! What can they hope to gain?"
Roz could hear the thread of hysteria in her voice, but
she couldn't help it. Every time she turned around,
they were being attacked.

She felt Jamie come up behind her and rest his
hands on her shoulders. Just the contact calmed her.
She touched one of his hands.

"Why do they want Crumpet so badly?"

Jamie studied the note. "We're not playing with someone who has a full deck. There's no way the will can be changed, even contested. That's why they're asking you to meet with them, so they can make this deal. You have to realize you have all the power."

"I don't even *want* it! I feel like telling all three of them they can have the money if they'll just call off these people and leave Crumpet alone!"

"I don't think it's even a question of money anymore. You have to understand what it meant to all three of Matthew's children when he left his fortune to Crumpet. My mother didn't visit him much after he married Katherine. They didn't get along too well, because Mom doesn't put up with society bull. Katherine was always interested in how much money a person made, the right parties to attend, the perfect connection. Matthew knew he'd made a mistake by the third year they were married, but by that time Sarah had been born, and he didn't want to leave the children with Katherine."

"But why did they turn out so badly if they had Matthew for a father?" She had thought about so many aspects of Matthew's life while she'd walked the halls of the mansion. He had been heartbroken with the way his children had turned out, but he had never told her why it had happened.

"He never had a chance. Katherine was an emotional manipulator. Mom said she never saw anything like it. In those days, fathers went to work, and mothers stayed home. She had all three of the children thinking her way by the time they were in school."

"But Matthew—"

"Matthew was essentially alone. He had a few women that he saw on the side; he was never short of companionship during those days. But I know he wasn't happy about it. He would have preferred a real marriage, but Katherine made it impossible."

"Did he ever consider divorce?"

"Katherine claimed it was against her religion, but she just wanted to hold on to him and his money. I was always relieved she died before he did."

"So he never had a chance to love anyone. Not really." Roz felt her eyes begin to fill at the thought of the older man going through life alone. Jamie gave her shoulders a gentle nudge, and she realized he was encouraging her to lie down. She walked over to the bed and sat down, her legs unsteady. She felt so very tired. "Poor Matthew. I wish I'd come into his life at an earlier time. He used to be happy with the simplest little things."

Jamie sat down next to her, and Crumpet jumped up beside him. "I know he was happy with you, Roz. He used to talk about you to my mother. He never told her exactly how he met you, or I would have scratched you as a suspect long ago. Mom kept telling me you couldn't have possibly murdered him, but I had to consider that Matthew had fallen in love with Katherine. If he could be fooled once, the possibility remained he could be fooled again."

Roz looked down at her hands, then reached over and petted Crumpet. The bulldog rolled over so she could scratch his stomach, then sighed as she found the right spot.

"Matthew loved me. He wasn't *in* love with me."

"Don't kid yourself, Roz. If you'd been just a little older—you were the light of his life. You and Crumpet."

She closed her eyes tightly. "I hate what the money is doing to everyone, Jamie. Couldn't we offer to give some of it back to them? Or the houses and apartments? I'd give anything to just be able to leave the house and take a walk without looking over my shoulder."

"It won't be much longer. They've been pretty clumsy so far. If we were dealing with experts, Crumpet would have been dead by now."

The subject of their conversation began to bark furiously, and Roz reached for the remote control and changed the channels until she found a movie. *The Wizard of Oz* had just started, and she watched as Crumpet ran up to the screen and sat directly in front of it.

"Won't he bark at Toto?"

"This was one of Matthew's favorite films. He used to watch it every year, and he'd hush Crumpet up. Watch, he won't make a sound."

Crumpet looked as if he'd been carved from stone.

Roz turned back toward Jamie. "Tell me more about the children. I have a feeling I'm going to need all the help I can get tomorrow."

"They're master manipulators. They believe they're above ordinary people; at least that's what Katherine always told them. Presenting the proper social facade was everything. That's what I meant to tell you earlier. It must have killed all three of them to have the tabloids sensationalizing Matthew's will. All it did was shout to the world he cared so little about them he gave his fortune to a dog.''

"They would have never understood the relationship he had with Crumpet."

"How could they? The only meaningful relationship each of them has had is with themselves."

"Sarah married."

"Sarah and her husband lead separate lives. Mark is shuttled between them."

"No wonder he's a mess.'' She glanced at the clock, then closed her eyes. "I can't sleep. All I keep thinking about is that I have to meet with those horrible people."

"I'll be right beside you. You won't be alone. Even if you can't sleep, lie down and close your eyes. I'll watch Crumpet."

ROZ GOT UP with a sense of dread the next morning. She went jogging with Jamie and Crumpet to work off some of the tension gripping her body, then forced herself to drink a health shake. She spent the rest of the afternoon watching the clock, and at two-thirty she and Jamie and Crumpet walked out to his black Corvette.

She was silent for most of the drive. When Jamie finally parked the car, he reached across Crumpet and grasped her hand.

"Remember the part in the movie last night where Glinda told Dorothy the ruby slippers had to be very powerful for the bad witch to want them so badly?"

"Yeah." Her reply was short, terse. She was nervous, and nothing Jamie said was going to dispel her fears.

"Just think of Crumpet as a pair of ruby slippers. *You've* got the power, Roz. Don't let them make you forget it."

IT WAS A HORRIBLE AFTERNOON, one Roz would never forget as long as she lived. Jamie had been right—both Matt and Elizabeth were shocked when Crumpet walked in. The bulldog stayed close to Roz's heels. As soon as he saw Matthew's children, he strained away from them. Roz chose the chair farthest away and remained silent.

She didn't have to wait long. Elizabeth's color was high, and there was a desperate look in her eyes.

"Rosalind, this has gone far enough! You have to cooperate with us! I don't know how you can live in that house and take advantage of everything my father worked for all his life and feel you're doing the right thing."

Calm. Stay calm. "I'm simply doing what Matthew asked me to do in his will. I'm making sure Crumpet is well taken care of."

"You're *using* my father! You've moved all your horrid animals out there and turned my father's house into a *zoo*! There was nothing in his will that gave you permission to do that."

Roz remained silent.

"You answer me when I talk to you!" Elizabeth got out of her chair, and Roz fought the urge to leap to her feet and run. But then Jamie leaned back and let his jacket fall open, and Elizabeth caught a glimpse of his gun in the shoulder holster. She swallowed, then sat back down abruptly.

"Rosalind, I didn't think you'd resort to threats!"

"I'm not threatening you."

"Then why is that man beside you carrying a gun?"

Jamie answered her. "I'm an employee of Ms Locklear's. I'm only interested in her and Crumpet's protection. There have been several attempts on the dog's life, and she thought it best if Crumpet were accompanied by a bodyguard wherever he goes."

"That's the most ridiculous thing I've ever heard!"

Roz gave Elizabeth what she hoped was her most chilling glance. "I don't think Matthew would have enjoyed the prospect of Crumpet being killed. This man is licensed to carry a handgun, and he shoots to kill. Am I making myself perfectly clear?"

There was total silence in the office.

"Now, I have an appointment at four. Could you please get to the point of this meeting?"

Neither brother nor sister would look at each other. Finally, Elizabeth blurted out, "I need some of my money."

"Your father's money," Roz reminded her gently.

"I have bills that have to be paid."

Quietly, with as little fanfare as possible, Roz pulled a checkbook out of her purse. "How much do you need?"

"Three hundred thousand dollars."

Though inwardly she was wincing, Roz wrote the check with a steady hand. She tore it carefully out of the book, then entered the amount. The only sound in the room was Crumpet's anxious wheezing.

"Elizabeth, I'm giving you this check on the condition that you call off the people who are trying to kill Crumpet. It's getting to be a nuisance." She hoped she had just the right amount of annoyance in her voice and the woman wasn't seeing how upset she really was.

Elizabeth didn't say anything for a moment, then looked at Crumpet. Roz was chilled by the hatred in the woman's eyes.

"The day my father got that dog, I should have stuffed him in a bag and thrown him out on the freeway."

"Call them off, Elizabeth. You're not going to win this war."

"You have no right to that money!"

"This has nothing at all to do with me. When Crumpet dies—of natural causes—the money is going to go to a charitable cause and help animals all over the city. It was your father's dream, Elizabeth. He wanted to make a difference in some way. You and I have no right to tamper with his wishes."

"How easy for you to say, living in that house and spending his money."

"Ms Locklear hasn't spent anything beyond a modest household allowance," the lawyer pointed out.

"Shut up, Stewart! What the hell am I paying you for!"

"You get the check on the condition that you call off your goons. If you don't agree to my terms, I have no qualms about tearing this up." She waved the check in her hand.

"I don't like you, and I didn't like my father, and I *hate* that miserable dog!"

"My terms or no check. It's up to you." Roz almost shrank back against the palpable hatred coming at her. Crumpet was trembling at her feet, and she reached down with her free hand to give the dog a comforting pat.

"Damn you. All right, I'll meet your conditions. Now give me—"

Roz set the check down on the lawyer's desk, having no desire to hand it to Elizabeth. Then she stood up and walked out of the room with as much dignity as she could, considering Crumpet was pressed against her legs.

At the doorway, she turned back and fixed Elizabeth with a look she hoped radiated strength. "If you don't call off those men, I'll have no qualms about sending my bodyguard after you. And he doesn't like people who break their promises."

Her legs shook all the way to the car, and she didn't feel relaxed until the Corvette's doors were slammed shut and they were on the road.

"HE SHOOTS TO KILL?" Jamie was grinning as Roz climbed back into the car. They had driven into Hollywood afterward and stopped at Pink's on La Brea, the best chili-dog stand in the city.

"Here's your two chili dogs." She handed them over the shift to Jamie and then began to bite into her own.

"I'll have no qualms about sending my bodyguard after you." He started to laugh. "You were great; you should have seen the look on her face when you left the office. I think she's used to having the last word."

"Would you go after her if something happened to Crumpet?"

"In a minute."

"Then I wasn't really lying."

"It's true I don't like people who break their promises." He started to laugh again and had to set his chili dog down on the dash. "And to think I was worried about you in there!"

"I just got so mad! I kept thinking of all the times they tried to get Crumpet. When she said she wished she'd dumped Crumpet on the freeway, that's when I lost it."

"My favorite of all time will always be 'he shoots to kill.' Roz, I don't think it's Crumpet who's been watching too many movies."

"It worked, didn't it? Do you think she'll stop?"

"For now."

"Hey, what am I worried about? As long as she thinks you shoot to kill and I can keep making her believe we're on top of things, we've got a chance."

"More than a chance. I think this case is almost closed."

Chapter Eight

The attacks on Crumpet's life stopped as abruptly as
they had begun. Thanksgiving came and went, and
Roz opened Matthew's home to all the people she
knew who had no place to go. She and Jamie cooked
a dinner for twenty-four, two huge roast turkeys with
all the trimmings. They baked pies the day before, and
as Roz looked around the bright, warm kitchen, she
could almost put her fears to rest.

But she was still cautious.

Crumpet was never out of her sight unless he was
with Jamie. She began to work longer hours at the
shelter. The holidays sometimes depressed her, for it
seemed they brought out the worst in people. She did
all of her shopping by catalog this year, since she had
no desire to leave the mansion except to go to work.
She found spectacular presents for everyone. An an-
gora sweater her mother would love. Funny socks for
her coworkers at the shelter. They had cats and dogs
knitted into them, and crazily contrasting heels and
toes. All the dogs received stockings she sewed and
filled with bones and toys. Eldin, the cat, got his usual
catnip mouse. He had taken to living with Jesse, and

Roz was almost tempted to ask her friend if he wanted the fluffy orange cat for Christmas.

She kept up with Matthew's charities, working at his desk in his study and writing checks for the usual generous amounts. She sent out very few Christmas cards, mostly to people she had met when she and Deena had moved across the country. And she wrote her mother a long, newsy letter filled with everything but the attacks on Crumpet and the unpleasantness of Matthew's children.

It was still a difficult time for her. By nature and necessity a loner, Roz found it difficult to be either confined or always in someone's company. She still had strong feelings for Jamie, but sometimes she longed to be able to take a walk by herself, to get away from everything and everyone.

One morning, she suggested this to him.

"We still have to be careful, Roz. The only thing making me nervous is the unstable element. I don't trust Elizabeth, and I certainly don't believe her."

"I'm asking for just an hour of time. I won't leave the grounds. I need to have time by myself, and I feel that if I don't get out of the house and do some thinking, I'll go crazy!"

Though he wasn't pleased by her request, he granted it. She would never have gone against his wishes, for she had promised to let him know exactly where she was at all times. Even though the last few weeks had been quiet, Roz was sensible enough to realize they still had to be cautious.

Kai and Sting tried to join her, bouncing around at her heels, but she shooed them back toward the house. She needed the time alone. There had been several things troubling her, and walking alone always helped her to think.

It was an overcast day, the sky gray and cloudy. There had been a light drizzle that morning, so as Roz turned the collar of her jacket up and began to walk briskly away from the mansion, she decided not to go too far. There was a path lined with tall pine trees Matthew had planted, and she headed toward it. The trees were tall and thick enough to shut a person off from the rest of the world, and that was exactly what she felt like.

The needles crunched underneath her boots as she started down the path, and she breathed in the sweet air deeply. Matthew had created his own little paradise outside, a means of coping with the pressures of his business. The two of them had walked this path many times. The gazebo was at the end of it, and though she didn't intend to go that far or be gone that long, she decided to walk halfway down the path and then turn back.

She knew she had followed Matthew's wishes to the letter, thus far, and that was what was important to her. Crumpet was safe, living at the estate. The money was going to be given to a worthy cause. Matt and Elizabeth had been thwarted—for now. Sarah was in England, visiting relatives on her mother's side of the family for the holidays; and her son, Mark, was with his father in Malibu. So the children were accounted for. And, most important, since the day at the lawyer's office, no one had tried to kill Crumpet.

But how long can it last? She knew Crumpet was only five years old. He still had several good years left before old age caught up with him. And Roz was sure the battle with the Barrett children would last as long as she lived in their father's home. She didn't know if she had the strength to cope with it that long.

And then there was Jamie. He was confident the killer was going to slip up, or he was going to come across something in his investigation that would reveal what had really happened the night Matthew died. All of his children had had airtight alibis, but Roz was sure Elizabeth had been involved. She knew none of Matthew's children had possessed the slightest inkling of what the will contained; they had been too shocked at the reading.

It was still only a matter of time.

She tried to still her mind, to concentrate on the beauty around her and find some inner peace. That was something she'd had too little of. The tension inside her mounted day by day. Even though Jamie slept in the same bed with her, she still had trouble relaxing. Sometimes she wondered if he was still attracted to her, then quickly realized there were too many problems surrounding both of them to even consider beginning an intimate relationship.

She continued walking, but her steps slowed. Something wasn't right. It was too quiet. Usually there were birds and insects making noise. Even though it was damp, she'd still hear birds. She stood still and listened. Nothing.

The hair on the back of her neck started to rise, and her hands trembled. *You're scaring yourself—stop it.* Yet she clenched her fingers into fists and turned, then began walking quickly back toward the main house.

When she heard footsteps behind her, she lost all control and started to run. The cold air hurt her lungs, and her boots felt heavy on her feet. The footsteps sounded louder now; there was no attempt being made to hide their sound. Panicked energy burst through her body, and she forced her legs to keep moving.

The hand that grabbed her hair and jerked her to a standstill was far from gentle. Leather-gloved fingers slammed against her mouth, and she tasted her own blood. The other hand let go of her hair and then wound itself around her waist and seemed to be slowly squeezing the breath out of her.

"You think you're pretty smart, don't you." The whisper was a half rasp, the voice hard. "Well, you didn't say anything about hurting you, only the dog."

It was impossible to say anything with the gloved hand pressed tightly against her mouth. Her throat was so constricted, she doubted she could have, anyway. Her heart was hammering wildly, and she looked up at the pearl-gray sky. Only minutes ago everything had seemed so peaceful and serene. Now she was caught in a nightmare.

"Give up the dog, Rosalind. If you know what's good for you, let the dog go. And don't go lending Elizabeth any more money, because—"

"You want the dog, not her. Get your hands off her before I have to kill you."

She could have wept when she heard Jamie's voice. She could feel the tension in the man behind her as he loosened the grip around her waist. His hand dropped away from her mouth, and she took a deep breath, then dug her nails into her palms to steady herself. She couldn't faint. Not now.

"Walk away from him, Roz. Quickly. Down the path to the house."

There was a cold edge to his voice, and she obeyed it instinctively.

"Don't look back. Keep walking."

She half walked, half jogged. She wanted desperately to glance back and make sure Jamie was safe, but she did as he'd told her and continued down the needle-strewn path.

When the gunshot exploded into the still morning air, she fell to her knees and put her hands over her ears, closing her eyes tightly.

Jamie. Oh, Jamie.

She felt his arms around her waist within the minute, and she stumbled to her feet with his aid. Then she wrapped her arms around him and hugged him fiercely against her.

"Oh, God, I thought he'd killed you." The words were almost sobbed out.

"Are you all right?" She felt him running his hands over her body quickly, checking her. "Did he hurt you?"

"No. No, I'm all right. Is he—" She glanced down the path, then quickly looked away.

"He decided to use his gun. He was pointing it at you."

She pressed her hand against her mouth, then stumbled to the side of the path and threw up her breakfast. Jamie held her as she was sick and afterward drew a handkerchief out of his pocket for her to wipe her mouth.

"Let's get you home." He picked her up and began to walk down the silent path.

"I can walk—"

"Your legs are shaking."

He carried her into her bedroom and set her down carefully. She was still shaking as he tore one of the blankets off the bed and wrapped it around her. Then he eased her into his lap and held her tightly.

"Crumpet—"

"He's with Jesse. Five minutes after you left, I started to have bad feelings."

They were silent, and she knew he was thinking about what might have happened if he hadn't followed her.

When he finally spoke, his voice sounded drained. "No more walks, Roz. I'm so sorry."

THERE WAS NO ATTEMPT on her part to be happy that evening. Jamie fixed her a spinach and Monterey Jack cheese omelet with fried potatoes, and she pushed the food halfheartedly around her plate before giving up and feeding it to Rocky.

She went to bed early but couldn't sleep. Every time she closed her eyes, she kept seeing the pathway, hearing the gunshot. Her mind kept returning to what she'd seen before she'd quickly averted her gaze.

Jamie had killed a man.

She didn't feel sorry for her attacker; she knew Jamie had given him a chance to come with him quietly. But she wondered who would be insane enough to send someone so trigger-happy after her.

The nightmare was beginning to close in, suffocating her. When Jamie had mentioned he thought they might go after her, that was all it had been. A thought. What had happened on that path this morning had been real life. And death.

She felt the mattress dip slightly and opened her eyes. Jamie was sitting on the far end. His fingers were deftly removing another cigarette from the pack, and she knew he was upset.

She levered herself up, supporting her weight on her elbow. "Are you all right?"

"Yeah."

She slid up in bed and moved closer. He'd picked up the book of matches and was trying to light the cigarette, but his hand was shaking. It was the slightest movement, but she saw it, and it affected her, striking straight to the heart of her emotions.

"Oh, Jamie." She gathered him in her arms and hugged him tightly.

He threw the pack of matches and cigarette down, and she felt his arms come up around her, crushing her against his chest. His words were muffled against her hair, but she heard the agony in his voice.

"If I hadn't followed you—if he'd had you alone for only a few minutes more—"

"No, don't think about that. You were the one who told me you can drive yourself crazy thinking that way. We're in this together, right?"

"Roz, every time I close my eyes, I see him."

"I know," she whispered. "Me, too."

"I think it's becoming too dangerous." He took a deep breath. "I may ask you and Crumpet to go away for a while. I talked to my mother on the phone today, and she said you could fly up there. She'd be happy to—"

"No..." He started to speak again, and she put her fingers gently against his lips. "We're in this together all the way. I wouldn't feel right, knowing you were alone in this house.''

''I can take care of myself.''

''That's not the point.''

''Roz, if anything happened to you—''

''Nothing's going to happen. I'm not going to take any more walks until this thing is finished. I don't need my solitude that badly.''

They were silent for a time, holding each other closely, until Roz whispered, ''I was never so scared as when I thought you were dead.''

''He was insane, pulling that gun on you.''

''You know what I kept thinking?'' She wet her lips, her throat tightening with nervousness. ''I kept thinking how much I would have regretted dying on that path and never having made love with you.''

He was perfectly still next to her, and for a moment she thought she'd been too forward. But in the next instant she heard his reply.

''I was thinking the same thing this afternoon. All I kept thinking was that I'd never see you smile, never kiss you.''

Roz blurted out the rest of her thoughts before she lost her nerve. ''Well, I was kind of thinking... You know, we have all this time just sitting around and waiting, and so I thought—''

''You thought what?'' He was teasing her now.

''I thought maybe we could use the time to—I don't know what I'm saying, Jamie. What do you think?''

''I think you're on to something good. And I have a surprise for you.'' She was startled as he jumped out of bed and raced down the hall in the direction of his former bedroom. When he came back, he was carrying a handful of VCR tapes.

"What's that?" For a moment she panicked. Did he want her to watch X-rated films with him before they made love? She'd had enough surprises for today.

"These tapes contain almost fifteen hours of Busby Berkeley films. If anything can keep Crumpet occupied, these can."

"You're really clever."

"I'll set the VCR up in my bedroom so he'll be close by; then I'll lock all the doors leading out to the hallway. He'll be safe, Roz; he'll be in the next room. He'll just be—out of the way."

"Am I objecting?"

He was back in bed in record time.

"Somehow I didn't picture our first time like this," Roz whispered as he slid over beneath the covers and pulled her against him. "I thought I'd be wearing something more romantic than my flannel nightgown."

"I'm not complaining."

When he slowly eased her nightgown over her head and dropped it by the side of the bed, Roz knew she had to tell him.

"Jamie, there's something I think you should know."

"I have no communicable diseases, and yes, I'll take care of it."

"That's not what I meant!"

He stopped touching her, and levering himself up on one elbow, looked down at her. "Is something wrong?"

"Sort of."

"What do you mean, sort of?"

"It's just—remember when I told you I didn't have a lot of social experience?"

"Roz, believe me, social experience is the last thing I'm thinking about right now."

She could feel his anxiety, and she touched his cheek gently. "I just don't want this to be a bad experience for you."

"It won't be. I'm ninety-nine percent sure this is going to be a trip to the moon for both of us."

She hesitated.

"I don't mean to rush you, but we have only fifteen hours of movies on that tape, and Crumpet could get bored of people dancing down gigantic cakes."

"Oh, Jamie—remember the night we danced out on the terrace?"

"Roz, I'm horrible at stuff like this. Could you just tell me?"

She leaned forward and whispered in his ear.

When she lay back down on the mattress, he was looking at her, his expression almost shocked.

"I'm sorry. I know it's not supposed to be fun for a guy to have to—"

"Fun? Roz, this goes a lot deeper than fun. I can't believe—wasn't there someone along the way, someone—"

"I was never in one place long enough to make friends. Then, when I left my mother, I had to work really hard to support myself. There was never any time."

"But you're—I mean, I can't believe a guy wouldn't—" He stopped, and she was surprised to see a blush creeping up his neck.

"We don't have to if you don't want to."

"I'm sorry; I'm handling this like an idiot. I guess I'm nervous. I've never been to bed with a virgin before." He pulled her against him and kissed her forehead. "I just want it to be good for you."

"It will be, Jamie. That's why I think I waited for you. I've never felt like this about anyone before, and this seems so right."

"That's the way I feel." He was silent for a moment; then she felt his hand close over her hips, and his fingers began to stroke her bare skin. "You don't know how many times I've lain in that bed and had fantasies about you."

"Really? About me? I never thought anyone would want to fantasize about me."

"I did." He was slowly easing the covers away from her body. She was naked now, and he was still dressed. She could feel her face growing hot as he looked at her body. Then he smiled down at her, and she knew deep inside that everything was going to be fine.

"You're just like I imagined you'd be. You have the softest skin, just like a peach."

She linked one of her hands with his, their fingers entwined. "Would you mind if this time we went really slow? I mean, to give me time to get used to everything."

"We'll take it as slow as you want." He gathered her into his arms, then whispered into her ear, "Remember when we were dancing out on the terrace? Well, it's sort of like that. This time I'll lead, and you just follow. It'll feel the same as when you forgot you were dancing and just moved your feet. There's no big secret." He kissed the tip of her nose.

"It's really that easy?" She wanted to believe him, didn't ever want him to regret this moment.

"Well, there is one secret." She looked quickly up into his face and saw that his blue eyes were warm, caressing. "It helps a hell of a lot, it always makes it so much better, when the two people involved love each other."

The bedroom was so quiet she could hear the clock ticking.

"Do you love me?" She could barely squeak the words out.

"Ah, Roz." He kissed her cheek. "If I'd had any doubts, they would have been left behind on the path this morning." He kissed her eyelids, her cheek, her temples. She felt his lips move slowly to the base of her throat, and her eyes opened wider.

"Your heart's pounding," he said softly.

"I guess that's because I love you, too." Something deep inside her, something sweet and precious, was released as she said the words. She had always hesitated before, perhaps knowing instinctively she would be hurt in the end, that there wasn't the same feeling from the other person. But this time she was sure.

"Just love me, Roz. Love me as much as I love you and we'll never have to come back down."

SHE WOKE UP THE NEXT MORNING and stretched contentedly, then buried her face in the pillow. It smelled like Jamie, and she smiled.

Love had made all the difference. He had been so tender with her, had brought her along so carefully. When each moment had happened, she'd been ready, eager to share herself with him and love him. When their bodies had merged, it had seemed to her something deeper was happening, that they had been headed toward that final culmination from the moment they'd first seen each other. She had been comfortable with him, as if she'd known him a long time ago.

Afterward, she'd snuggled up against him, and they'd talked. Not about what they'd just shared. Little things. She had tickled his toes with hers; he had ruffled her hair and kissed the back of her neck. As they continued to talk, she'd told him what being so close to him had felt like. And she'd felt joy flood every part of her body when he had admitted it felt the same way for him.

How had she lived before Jamie, before knowing this closeness? She felt she could conquer anything right now, as if the world were back on the right path and it was only a matter of time before she, Jamie and Crumpet would be able to go on with their lives.

And deep inside she knew the three of them would be together.

"Hungry?"

She sat up among the sheets as she heard his voice, then couldn't stop smiling when she saw him standing in the doorway, a breakfast tray in hand.

"Crumpet decided to wake me up this morning. So I thought you might like some French toast."

"French toast? I thought omelets were your specialty."

"I made you one last night." He set the tray down over her knees and gave her a quick kiss. "That's okay. Champ and Sting enjoyed eating my disasters. But none for Crumpet.''

As if he were answering his name, Roz heard Crumpet barking as he ran down the hall; then the bulldog tore into the bedroom and began to race around the room.

''Crumpet! Settle down! Jamie, what's wrong with him?''

''I just told him, 'Crumpet, I want you to act out how I'm feeling this morning.' '' When she started to laugh, he said, ''No, I think he's just excited because he thinks he's going to get some of this French toast.''

''Silly dog.''

''Or it's a movie overdose.''

She never remembered a happier breakfast. They sat in bed and laughed and drank coffee. Crumpet bounded up on the bed, and Roz fed him a little bite of her breakfast. Then Jamie put the tray on the bedside table and took her into his arms.

''No regrets?''

''Not one.''

''I'm glad.''

He kissed her. She softened her mouth beneath his and tugged on his hair gently. When he broke the kiss, he looked down into her eyes.

''The subtle approach doesn't work with me, Peach. You're going to have to be blunt.''

She was delighted with the nickname. ''I thought maybe—''

''With all the time we have in the house—''

''And I don't have any errands to run.''

''And Crumpet still has four more movies to watch.''

"And it's so close to Christmas."

"And peaches like to be squeezed."

"It was just a thought."

"And people who are crazy in love with each other like to spend a lot of time making love." He finished the discussion by covering her mouth with his.

THE HOLIDAYS WERE MAGICAL. They bought an enormous blue spruce and set it up in the library. Presents began to appear mysteriously beneath its branches. They baked cookies and laughed, and both of them made time to take several turkeys to the Skid Row Mission in downtown Los Angeles.

Crumpet loved Christmas. He destroyed several rolls of wrapping paper, patrolled the kitchen, watching for pieces of cookie dough to fall on the floor, and tried to tear down the tree. He discovered one of the doggie stockings and shredded it throughout the long hallway, then chewed up the bone and thundered through the house after the hard rubber ball.

Everyone was in a holiday mood, and Roz could not remember enjoying a Christmas more.

They opened their presents on Christmas Eve.

"This is the way we've always done it in my family," Jamie said.

"Oh, sure. You just can't control yourself. You're just like Crumpet. You have to make sure you know what's in every present."

"Not true. I think there are a couple I haven't investigated."

"Yeah, the ones you bought."

She howled with laughter when he opened his present from Crumpet: *1001 Ways with Omelets*. She was touched when he gave her a gift from the dog. *A History of the English Bulldog.* Champ's leg had healed completely, and he and the other dogs lay around the tree, chewing their rawhide-strip bones. Rocky slept peacefully in her bathroom, a blue plastic bone between her paws.

"The best for last," Jamie announced as he reached underneath the tree and unearthed another package.

Roz opened it quickly, then stared at the hardcover book. It was a mystery, and as she studied the cover, she realized it was his father's newest, due out in March.

"Oh, Jamie, thank you!"

"Open up the cover."

It was autographed. "To Rosalind, a heroine in her own right. I hope to meet you soon. Sincerely, Alan Cameron."

"Jamie, this is wonderful."

"Dad thought you showed exceptionally good taste."

"You haven't opened yours yet. I hope you like it."

"Anything you get me, Peach, will be wonderful."

She was nervous until she saw his reaction. She had had a snapshot she'd taken of Matthew and Crumpet enlarged, then bought an elegant brass frame. She had snapped it one summer day in the gazebo and had always liked the photo, because both man and dog looked so happy.

The expression on Jamie's face was exactly what she'd hoped for.

"This is the way I always want to remember him, with that little smile on his face."

"I took it the first summer I met Matthew. We went on a long walk that day, and he and Crumpet just collapsed on the bench. Then Crumpet crawled into his lap and licked his face, and I caught it just as Matthew looked down at him."

"It's beautiful, Roz. I'd like to get a copy made for my mother. She'll cry when she sees it."

"Then that's it."

"There's one more thing. I think it's right over here."

She hadn't noticed the small silver box hanging from one of the branches. When Jamie took it down and handed it to her, she felt as if all the breath left her lungs at once.

"Open it up."

Her fingers seemed disconnected from her brain, but she finally managed to open the small box. Inside was a silver ring.

"I bet you never went steady with anyone, either."

She couldn't speak.

"I hope this doesn't mean no."

"No—I mean, yes."

He slipped the ring on her finger, and it sparkled in the light. She couldn't stop looking at it.

"What it means is, we're now exclusive."

She could only stare at him and was surprised to see he was nervous.

"I don't want to rush you into anything, Roz, so I thought we could take it a step at a time. I mean, we could be together for a while, and you could discover things about me you could never live with."

"Like the way you make French toast or something."

"Exactly."

She moved closer to Jamie. "I don't think that's going to happen."

"I think you're probably right."

Later that evening, as they watched a Christmas special with Crumpet, and Roz poured them both their last glass of eggnog, Jamie nudged her.

"Don't make any sudden moves, but look at the bathroom."

Rocky was lying in the doorway, her head on the bedroom carpet. Her large, sad brown eyes were trained on the television set. Her Christmas bone was between her paws, and she looked more relaxed than Roz had ever seen her.

"And people don't believe in miracles," Roz said softly.

It was a Christmas filled with miracles for Roz, the most important being that for the first time in her life she felt emotionally, spiritually and physically connected to someone. She had come full circle and had learned to trust and love Jamie. She was able to lean on him and share her troubles as well as her happiness. As she lay in bed with him, curled up against the warmth of his body and feeling his arms around her, she wondered how she had ever thought her life was complete before.

The fire was glowing softly, sending shadows flickering over the bedroom ceiling as they talked. More than anything, Roz realized this was what had been lacking in her life, the quiet intimacy of lovers talking underneath the covers.

Jamie kissed her cheek softly. "You were absolutely right about Rocky. How did you know? I never thought she'd survive, and here she is, venturing out of the bathroom."

"It's just a feeling I get when I first see an animal. It's kind of hard to explain."

"What did you feel when you first saw me?"

"I liked the way you took off your jacket and got right in and picked up a kitten."

"And let it throw up on me. I remember you commented on that."

"You were kind, Jamie. That impressed me. What did you think about me?"

"I thought you had the nicest legs I'd ever seen in jeans."

"Besides stuff like that."

"Hey, we're talking about some of the basic reasons the species has survived."

She pinched his side gently, and he swatted her hand.

"What else?"

"I wanted to see you smile that special smile for me."

"What smile?"

"That really soft smile. It's slow, the way it comes onto your face, but it's a real smile, up in your eyes and everything."

"I don't know what you mean."

"You smiled that way when you first saw Rocky in the door."

"Oh."

"You smile that way after I kiss you."

"I do?"

"Yeah. I can't believe I used to actually be jealous of Crumpet because he made you smile. I was determined to get you to smile that way at me."

"I'll remember that. I'll have to make sure I give you your smile quota so you'll always feel good."

"You make me feel good all the time."

She snuggled against him and kissed his chin. "There's a musical on in about fifteen minutes. It's not Busby Berkeley, but I know Crumpet enjoyed it the last time he saw it."

"Are you coming on to me?"

"No, I just thought I might like to go into your room and watch it with him." She shrieked as he rolled them over quickly so his body was pinning hers to the mattress.

"Crumpet told me he wanted to watch it alone. It's an introspective film, and it makes him ponder the meaning of life."

She was still laughing when he kissed her.

Chapter Nine

"Tell me what the *T* stands for," Roz called as she batted the beach ball into the air. She and Jamie were swimming in the pool, while Crumpet sat on one of the chaise lounges and snoozed.

"You have to guess."

"I think steady girlfriends are entitled to know their boyfriend's initials."

"I think girlfriends should humor their boyfriends and guess."

"Thomas?"

"Too common."

"Ted?"

"Stuffy."

"Trent?"

"Nope." He dove underneath the surface, and seconds later she felt his fingers around one of her ankles. But he didn't pull her underwater, simply swam through her legs.

When he surfaced, she called out, "You're trying to distract me."

"Desperately."

"Is it a last name-first name? Like Trevor or something?"

"I wish it were."

"You don't like it?"

"You're catching on. I've insisted everyone call me Jamie for years."

"I'm not going to give up on this one."

"You'll never guess it."

"Worse than Rosalind?"

"A million times."

She guessed for a few minutes more, then swam to the shallow end of the pool and walked up the cement steps. She headed toward Crumpet and when she reached him, called out cheerfully, "Turn over, Crumpet."

The bulldog rolled on his back and waved his paws in the air. Roz put both her hands underneath his body and rolled him to the other side. Reaching underneath the chaise, she pulled out the small plastic bottle of sunscreen and poured some into her hands. She applied it carefully to Crumpet's face, making sure each wrinkle was protected, and especially his broad black nose. Then she rubbed more of the solution over his side and down his legs. The bulldog's fur was so short he had actually been sunburned before, so Dr. Ramsey had suggested using a high-SPF sunscreen when he was out in the sun for long.

"All he needs is a pair of sunglasses and a pool phone and he can start directing movies," Jamie said, still in the middle of the Olympic-size pool.

"Knowing Crumpet, it would be a musical."

"Bad move, Crumpet. Production costs would be too high. You should go with a short, meaningful drama."

"But he hates that kind of movie. He always falls asleep."

"Think of something you could shoot right around here. Like *Dynasty*."

They were still laughing and talking when Jamie looked toward the house and said softly, "Don't look now, but one of the children is here." He swam quickly to the shallow end and climbed out of the pool. She watched him as he threw a towel over his broad shoulders, then sat down by the beach bag he'd brought outside with them.

She knew his shoulder holster was inside.

She looked away as he reached inside the bag, not wanting reality to intrude on such a pleasant afternoon. But it was impossible to forget once she started thinking about it. She began to walk toward the cement steps.

"Hello, Sarah. Hi, Mark."

Sarah was elegant as usual, and Roz had to admire her style. Where Elizabeth was usually upset and flustered or spewing venom, nothing seemed to mar Sarah's classically beautiful face. This time, Roz noted she sat at one of the tables farther away from the pool. Mark stood awkwardly at her side, as if awaiting further instructions.

"Crumpet, stay," Roz said quietly as she passed the dog. He rolled over on his side, and a part of her mind noticed his hair was standing up on his back. Whether from the sunscreen or because one of the Barretts was here, it was hard to tell. She picked up another large beach towel as she passed Jamie's table and wrapped it around her body, sarong style.

"Don't let her get to you. Remember the ruby slippers," he whispered.

"What's she doing here? She didn't call."

"I'll be watching her the entire time. You have nothing to worry about." He snapped his fingers. "C'mere, Crumpet. I don't want you out in the open."

The bulldog trotted over and obediently sat at his feet.

Roz tried to put enthusiasm in her step as she walked over to Sarah and her son. She sat down in the chair across from her, then signaled to Maria, who was standing on the top terrace, watching.

After they'd both requested drinks, Roz leaned back and said carefully, "I hope you enjoyed England over the holidays."

"It was wet. I missed California."

Though the words were friendly, Roz felt something was out of place. It was the strangest sensation. There were so many times she felt the outer conversation didn't match what was really going on. She was used to watching for body-language clues in the animals, and the skill had translated itself over into her conversations with people. Sarah's conversation felt wrong.

Roz decided to let Sarah bring up what it was she wanted. Leaning back in the chair, she waited.

It didn't take long. "I talked with my sister the morning I returned."

Roz simply smiled.

"She told me you wrote her a check. That was a very thoughtful thing to do."

Roz tried not to let her surprise show on her face. A Barrett thanking her for something? This was a first.

"But that's what I came to talk to you about. My sister has a definite problem with money. I think the only way she's ever going to be able to control herself is if she realizes she has to be responsible for her actions. Every time you bail her out, you'll only be giving her permission to run up more bills."

"I see."

"I talked with Mr. Rissman, our lawyer, when I came back. He told me your expenses still continue to be minimal. I'm impressed."

Still wary, Roz said, "Thank you."

"Matt is too much of an autocrat, and Elizabeth gets too emotional. If there's to be any hope of communication, it has to be between the two of us."

"That sounds reasonable to me."

"You can understand my concern. I certainly wouldn't want my sister to spend all the money by the time my son is ready to collect his inheritance."

"I can understand that."

"My sister is capable of doing that. She's run through enormous sums before this."

"I wasn't aware of that. Thank you for informing me." She saw no point in telling Sarah that Matthew had told her about Elizabeth's experiments with drugs and her costly cocaine habit.

"Then we understand each other?"

"Yes."

"The other question I have is of a more personal nature."

"Oh?" This conversation was definitely making her uneasy.

"I promised Mark he could have a puppy when we got back from London. Would you happen to have any in your shelter right now?"

Roz glanced at Mark. She was always careful to make sure that the children she gave animals to were emotionally well equipped to take care of them. It was a sad truth, but sometimes children could be crueler than adults.

"What kind of a dog would you like, Mark?"

She was touched by the hopeful look in his eyes. They were warm and brown, not his mother's cool blue. She wondered what his father looked like.

"I want one like Crumpet."

She almost laughed out loud at the quick look of distaste that passed over Sarah's cool features. "That may be a little bit of a problem. We don't usually get pedigreed bulldogs in on a regular basis."

"But I like the way he snorts."

"Mark," Sarah scolded. "I'm sure you can find—"

"Mark, why don't you go over and pet Crumpet and let me talk to your mom for a minute, okay? We'll see what we can do to get you your bulldog." She had caught something in the child's eyes that had reminded her of her own childhood. At least she had felt somewhat secure with Deena, even if they had moved around a lot. This child, shuttled between two parents who led their own lives and looked out for their own interests, needed a four-legged friend. She was a firm believer in the qualities a pet could bring out in a child.

As Mark ran over to where Jamie was sitting, Roz turned back to Sarah. "I know several breeders I can contact for you if you'd like. Bulldogs are excellent dogs for children; they're gentle and smart."

"I'm not sure I like the idea." Sarah gave Roz a cool look. "I can't pretend I like the dog." As she said this, she glanced over toward Crumpet and Roz followed her gaze. She smiled as she saw Mark gently patting Crumpet's head. Jamie was talking to him, and the boy looked truly happy for the first time Roz could remember.

Why did she have the niggling feeling those were the first honest words out of Sarah's mouth? What was she trying to accomplish, coming here and talking pleasantly? Surely she had to realize they could never be anything but polite strangers. Unless fate had thrown her into contact with the Barretts, Roz was sure she would never have had the desire to know any of them.

"Let me call a few breeders. If that doesn't work out, we have a litter that should be ready in about three weeks."

"And what kind are they?"

"A mixed bunch. I think there's some collie, shepherd and maybe Saint Bernard."

"Mark can't have a mixed breed. I want him to have a pedigreed animal."

Then why come to me? "I'll talk with my vet and see if he knows of any purebred puppies in the area."

"Thank you, Rosalind; you've been most kind. And thank you for the iced tea." Rising gracefully to her feet, Sarah shaded her eyes against the bright afternoon sun and said, "Mark, we have to go!" She glanced back at Roz. "Would you mind if we use the bathroom? I can't stand it when his hands aren't clean."

Roz forced a smile. "No problem." Mark needed a dog, needed anything that would help him spend time with someone besides his mother.

After they left, she joined Jamie at his table.

"What did she want?"

"She didn't want me to give Elizabeth any more checks."

"As much as I hate to admit it, she's probably right. Elizabeth spends in one day what you'd spend in a couple of years running this place."

"She wanted a dog for Mark. He wants a bull-dog."

"He's a nice kid. Overpowered by his mother but a nice kid. I think a dog might be good for him."

"I do, too. It was a strange conversation. She was saying all the right things, but it didn't add up."

"How do you mean?"

"It didn't feel right."

"Did you feel threatened?"

"No. Just that what she was saying wasn't what she really wanted to say."

"You're smart not to trust her. Matthew stopped trusting any of them when they were quite young."

Roz tilted her head back and closed her eyes, letting the sun bathe her face. "I will not let her ruin my day." She took a deep breath, then let it out slowly, trying to relax. "Would you like to barbecue hamburgers on the terrace tonight?" Before the sentence was completed, she felt Crumpet's paws on her leg, and looking down, saw a pair of the most mournful eyes.

"I take it *hamburger* is in his vocabulary, too."

She laughed and pushed thoughts of Sarah out of her mind.

ROZ DECIDED to have a small New Year's party. When she found out her mother and Harold were going to be in town, she invited them. She asked Dr. Ramsey, as she knew his wife had died several years ago and he would probably be spending the evening alone. Even Jesse, who usually opted for any number of wilder parties, decided to stay at the mansion that evening.

She was in the kitchen, making up a shopping list, when Jamie walked in. He was wearing casual pants and a sweater, with a loose jacket.

"I like that jacket," she commented.

"My mom gave it to me a couple of years ago." He leaned over and gave her a quick kiss. "Is there anything you want me to pick up?"

"Jesse and I are going to leave in about an hour. Where are you off to?"

"I'm having lunch with a reliable source. The woman used to live next door to Matthew and Katherine when they lived in Beverly Hills. Jennings remembered her, and when I called her up, she said she would talk to her friends and see what she could come up with." He grinned. "There's nothing more organized than a society matron's gossip. I'm sure some of it will be useful."

"Just make sure you get back in time for the new year."

"This shouldn't take longer than an hour."

"If she's nice and has nowhere else to go, bring her back. We'll have plenty of food."

"Another stray, huh?" He kissed the top of her head. "You be careful."

"As always."

THE OUTDOOR CAFÉ was busy and noisy, and boasted excellent food as well as opportunities to see people and be seen. Jamie had the feeling that Olivia Stewart was a regular. She was a gossip of the first order. Olivia could remember dates and places and complete pieces of dialogue. Jamie suspected she had nothing else to do with her life. She was extremely helpful with details, and he was sure she wasn't embellishing her stories.

"You really ought to write a book. You've got the makings of several best-sellers here."

She fluttered her well-preserved hands, and the large diamond-and-emerald ring on her left hand flashed in the warm sunlight. "I wouldn't know how to go about doing that. I don't even know if I could."

"I'm sure you have people who could help you once the book was written. But if you have any questions along the way, you could call my father."

Once he explained who his father was, Olivia became enthusiastic.

"Do you really think I could do it?"

"I know you could. Some of those stories are too good. It'd be a shame if they never saw print."

"Young man, you've inspired me. I'm going to go straight to the computer store on Rodeo Drive and see how much a word-processing system costs—" She stopped talking abruptly and took Jamie's hand. "Look who just came in."

Jamie glanced up and saw Sarah winding her way past several of the outdoor tables. She glanced at them briefly, and Jamie saw absolutely no reaction pass over the aristocratic features.

"Does she know you?"

"Oh, heavens, yes. I used to talk with Matthew all the time over the fence. He was killing his rosebushes when I first met him, but I told him what Trudy did with hers and—"

Strange, Jamie thought. *You would think she would come over, if only for appearances.*

"—I used to tell Marvin, that girl always knew what she wanted and would do anything to get it. She drove her father to despair when she—"

"That's an interesting observation. I would have thought that about Elizabeth, but Sarah—"

"Oh, Jamie, no. You have to understand that family. It's always the cool personalities that boil underneath."

Jamie sat forward in his chair. His stomach was tightening, his instincts working overtime. "This is very important to me, Olivia. Take your time and tell me everything."

Within forty-five minutes, everything had fallen into place. Olivia seemed to want to stay and chat, so Jamie suggested she and her husband attend their New Year's party. He had to talk to Roz; then they were going straight to the police.

"You're a darling boy, Jamie, and I have to tell you I'll be on the phone all day tomorrow explaining to my friends what I was doing having lunch with a hand-some man young enough to be my son!''

Any other time he would have laughed, but now he had work to do. ''Olivia, let me walk you to your car. I'd love to chat, but I have another appointment, and I can't afford to be late.''

He paid the bill and escorted her out of the restaurant. But he forgot his jacket; it remained slung on one of the chairs.

It was a mistake he'd regret the rest of his life.

''JUST A MINUTE.'' Roz jumped up from the living room couch, swiping quickly at her eyes. She'd been reading another chapter in *A History of the English Bulldog*, and a particular story had started her crying. It had been the story Matthew always told her about the bulldog owned by a butcher. The man, betting with his friends, had cut off the dog's paws one by one, and she had still gone into the ring and fought. At the end, when the dog had pinned the bull, the butcher had severed his dog's head, and the crowd had roared.

''There are people like that,'' Matthew had told her wearily. ''I hope you never have to look pure evil in the face. It's an experience not soon forgotten.''

''Hang on!'' She swiped at her cheeks again, then wiped her hands on her jeans. Crumpet, who had been lying on the couch next to her, jumped down on the floor and followed her to the door.

''Who is it?'' she asked.

''Sarah. Oh, Roz, open the door. Something terrible has happened to Jamie!''

There was no mistaking the anguish in the woman's tone. Roz unbolted the door and let Matthew's daughter inside. She felt her stomach clench as she saw the jacket clutched in Sarah's hands. It was crumpled and dusty.

"What happened?" The moment had an air of unreality. She had just seen Jamie this morning, watched him walk out the door with that springy step she loved. She could still remember the look in his eyes when he'd leaned over the kitchen table and kissed her.

"He was hit by a car. He was having lunch with Olivia Stewart; it was an outdoor café. He walked her across the street to her car, and—"

"Is he all right?"

"They've taken him to the hospital. I didn't know who to contact as far as family, so I thought you could help me."

She couldn't keep her eyes off the jacket. She had to touch it. Sarah gave it to her, and she stared down at it. How could this have happened?

Crumpet jumped up against her leg, sniffed the jacket and whined.

"I'm coming with you. I have his mother's phone number in my purse. Oh, Sarah, was he terribly hurt?"

"I don't think he's going to die. But he was bleeding pretty badly."

She swallowed, fighting back the sick sensation in her stomach. Racing back to the kitchen, she grabbed her purse and Crumpet's leash. Then she followed Sarah out the front door and toward her silver Mercedes.

JAMIE WAS JUST PULLING OUT of his parking space when the bright orange Volkswagen barreled into his Corvette.

Damn! He jumped out of the car and darted to the back of the Corvette. The left fender was smashed in, but he barely gave it a glance.

"I'm so sorry, sir. I didn't see you leaving that space. Here, let me give you my home phone."

Too smooth. Most people yelled at the scene of an accident, tried to get out of responsibility, or were at least shaken up a little.

"Back it up, bud. This should cover your repairs." He reached for his jacket pocket, then suddenly realized his wallet was in his pants pocket.

My jacket. He had a sudden mental picture of it on the chair next to him, then saw Sarah walking through the outdoor tables, her face a perfectly smooth mask.

Something is very wrong. He didn't question his instincts.

"Move it! Move it or I'll have you arrested as an accomplice to a murder!"

The man's face paled. "Hey, man, she didn't tell me to *kill* you, just bang up your car."

He'd been right. "Just back up and get the hell out of here."

SARAH DROVE EXPERTLY through the winding Bel Air streets. Most of the estates had high fences and hedges, and Roz had gotten lost several times before because it was so hard to tell which direction she was going. It took her almost fifteen minutes before she realized they were climbing toward one of the canyons.

"What hospital did they take him to?" she asked.

"Cedars. I hope you don't mind, but I was supposed to be home for Mark. He's upset if I'm not there when he's driven home from piano lessons."

Privately, Roz thought Mark could have done without some of his mother's overprotectiveness. But now all her thoughts were centered around Jamie.

"You're sure he wasn't hurt that badly."

"I can't be positive, but I don't think he's going to die. Don't worry, Roz; we're almost there."

Within minutes, she turned into a driveway. The electronic gate parted smoothly, and the Mercedes swept up the circular drive.

"I shouldn't be longer than a minute. Why don't you come inside."

"I'll wait out here if you don't mind."

"I'm not asking you, Roz."

It took Roz a few seconds before she realized Sarah had a gun.

JAMIE POUNDED on the front door until his arm ached. When Maria answered it, she stared after him as he rushed past her into the hallway.

"Where's Roz?"

"She was in the living room, reading with Crumpet."

But all he found was the book Crumpet had given her for Christmas, neatly marked and on one of the couch cushions.

"Did she go to the market with Jesse?"

"No, she told me she decided to wait for you."

"Maria, get everyone together. I have to know where Roz is. This is very important—"

"She left with Sarah."

Oh, God. He wheeled around to find Tom in the doorway, a gardening trowel in his hand.

"She had your jacket in her hands. The one you wore this morning. And she was crying."

She had her. "Thank you, Tom. Tell Jennings to send some of his best men to this address." He scribbled Sarah's address frantically on a piece of paper. It was the only lead he had. "And, Maria, you pray."

"DID YOU POISON MATTHEW?" Roz asked quietly. She was standing in the middle of Sarah's living room, next to a marble coffee table with two bronze candlesticks on it. Crumpet was huddled behind her legs; she could feel the dog trembling. He was sensing her fear.

"I never loved my father; you knew that. He had time for everyone in the world but me. And I don't stand in anyone's shadow."

She didn't know if it was possible to reason with the woman, but she knew she had to try. Jamie couldn't help her this time. She had to get out of this alone.

"That must have hurt you very badly."

"I got over it. There's a lot money can buy. And I mean to have it all."

"What about Elizabeth and Matt?"

"You don't understand. Matt and Elizabeth don't have children. I have Mark to consider. He has to be brought up the proper way. It costs money. The right schools, the right clothing, the right connections. But you wouldn't understand any of that."

Sarah was Katherine reborn.

"Your bodyguard can't come rescue you now. I don't want to have to kill you, Rosalind. You're a sensible girl. I have a plan that can be beneficial to both of us. I get what I want for my son, and you stay alive."

"What is it?" She had to keep Sarah talking until she could think of a way to get the gun out of her hand.

"I've had some papers drawn up. You must know that you're in charge of making sure Matthew's money goes to those animal charities. But I'm sure you'll agree with me. I want you to do some creative book-keeping. I'm going to form a charity myself, and I want you to make sure that the bulk of my father's estate goes to it."

"I'm sure there would be no trouble with my doing that." Rosalind eyed the woman's face carefully, but she gave nothing away.

"There's only one little problem," Sarah continued.

Roz knew the problem was right behind her legs, shivering uncontrollably.

Sarah's voice was calm, cajoling. "Give me the dog, Roz. What's an animal like that to you? I'll set you up so well you'll be able to buy yourself ten bulldogs."

She could feel Crumpet's body pressed against her legs.

"Give me the leash. Let's not waste any more time."

Her mind flashed back to that afternoon in the garden with Matthew, and to Crumpet chasing butterflies.

Oh, Matthew, I failed you. I'm so sorry.

For a moment she thought he was in the room, she could remember his words so clearly.

Something that will demand all the courage you have, all of your heart and mind. Listen to that voice inside you. Take the reins and follow your heart.

And suddenly she knew, though she had always preserved life, that she would fight to the death to save Crumpet.

"Give me that leash." There was an edge to Sarah's voice, and Roz knew she wasn't a woman who was used to having orders disobeyed.

"What are you going to do with him?" *Pride. Katherine had a lot of pride.* She suspected Sarah would want to brag, too.

"I won't hurt him. The drug I have in mind will simply put him to sleep. It will look as if he dropped dead of heat exhaustion."

So you did kill Matthew. Suddenly Roz knew what he had meant about looking evil in the face. He had seen it take the form of his own flesh and blood.

"Wouldn't it make more sense to have him die at the mansion? Won't there be suspicion if he dies here?" She was surprised how calm her voice sounded, despite the fear twisting her insides.

"It won't look suspicious, because you'll say Crumpet had been behaving strangely. It's hot out today; he'll have run around in the garden. Come on, Rosalind; don't make this more complicated than it has to be. Give me the leash. You won't regret it, I promise you."

Throughout Sarah's impassioned speech, Roz had thought very strongly. A believer in animals being capable of picking up on visualized images in their training, she knew she had to somehow convey to Crumpet that things were going to be all right. The dog was still trembling, and she knew they both had to have their wits about them.

"Roz? I don't have all day."

It's all right. I'm here with you. I'm not going to give you to her. Never. Then, strangely enough, the image of Kai fighting with the masked intruder flitted into her thoughts.

"I knew you'd agree with me." Sarah reached out to take the leash from Roz's hands. As Roz felt her fingers brush over her wrist, she shuddered.

At that exact moment, Crumpet darted out.

He attacked Sarah's leg, and she screamed. Roz reacted quickly, bringing her hand down in a chopping motion she had once seen described on television. Her hand hit Sarah's wrist and the gun flew wildly.

Crumpet had set his massive jaws into her lower leg, and now he hung on as Sarah hopped around the room, screaming. Roz got down on her hands and knees and began to crawl as quickly as she could toward the gun.

But Sarah was faster. Roz heard a dull thud, then a yelp. Instinctively, she turned her head. It was a mistake. Sarah grabbed her by the hair, jerking her hand away from the gun.

Crumpet was lying very still on the white-carpeted floor.

Sarah tossed the bronze candlestick down beside him. Her leg was bleeding, and Roz shrank back. She had never seen such naked fury on a person's face before.

"That was a very stupid move on his part. It cost him his life."

She didn't say anything; she couldn't. She could only stare at Crumpet, lying on the floor.

"He could have been poisoned," Sarah began. "We could have had everything. Why did you try to take the gun out of my hand?"

Roz didn't answer. Crumpet was dead.

It seemed impossible that the bulldog would never get up again and race out into the garden to chase butterflies. Or wake her up with a sloppy kiss and wag his stumpy tail. He had been a part of her life for so long, a member of her family. And her last link to Matthew. She thought of the love and care she and Jamie had given Crumpet, only to have it all end because of Sarah's obsession to destroy.

She couldn't seem to feel anything. Her body was numb, light. It felt as if it belonged to someone else. The immense living room seemed to shrink in size. All she could do was stare at the still form of the bulldog and numbly remember that seconds ago he had been alive. And now Crumpet was dead, because he had defended her. He had tried to protect her from Sarah because he had loved her. With a quick flick of her wrist, Sarah had destroyed again, killing Crumpet as surely as she had killed her father.

She had always believed animals possessed souls, and the only consolation she had was that Crumpet was with Matthew now. If there was any justice in the afterlife, he would catch his butterflies and be happy. She looked up at Sarah, unable to face the still form of one of her dearest friends.

Crumpet, if you could fight, so can I. Roz abhorred violence of any kind, but now she had Sarah to face. This woman, who had killed her father and everything he had loved, did not deserve to win. Yet Roz knew the way the world worked, and there was a very good chance Sarah would succeed. With nothing but conviction on her side, Roz quietly faced her enemy. She would follow Crumpet's example. She wasn't a fighter in the physical sense of the word, but she would make the attempt. She couldn't give up now.

"You're a stupid little girl, Rosalind. I don't care how much my father loved you; you're nothing but white trash, and you don't deserve to live in my father's house!"

With absolutely nothing left to lose, Roz reached up and clawed Sarah in her face, raking her cheeks with her nails. The woman screamed, then pulled her hair backward until Roz thought her neck would snap. Her hands flailed wildly, and she felt the hem of Sarah's skirt. Yanking it, she caused Sarah to lose her balance, and the woman fell to the floor.

Roz wasn't a fighter, but she turned all her fury on Sarah, knowing she was fighting for her life. If she didn't win, Sarah would get away with killing both her and Crumpet. With Jamie in the hospital and all of Sarah's money, Roz knew it would be months before the case would even be considered.

Sarah was too clever. No one had suspected Matthew's murder, and she was sure the woman could make her and Crumpet's deaths look like accidents.

She bit Sarah's wrist hard as the woman tried to put her hand over her mouth. When Sarah's fingers started to squeeze against her throat, she bent her knee and kicked the woman.

Grunting, Sarah lost her advantage for precious seconds. Roz groped wildly, and her fingers closed over cold metal.

The gun.

She grasped it securely, and a part of her mind thought wildly, wondered if she could ever pull the trigger against another human being. But Sarah was beyond being human. She was a monster.

She had her fingers on the trigger when Sarah's hand slammed against hers, twisting her wrist cruelly.

In a reflexive action, she pulled the trigger, and the gun exploded in her hand.

JAMIE WAS JUST SLAMMING his car door when he heard the gunshot.

Roz. He closed his mind against what he might find, letting cold fury fill his body. Sarah had murdered Matthew. Sarah had been behind the man who had attacked Roz on the path. Sarah had been so clever, having Elizabeth set up the earlier attempts on Crumpet's life so that all suspicion would point toward the younger sister.

If Sarah had murdered Roz, he wasn't sure if he was capable of letting her out of that house alive.

"GET OVER ON THE BALCONY."

Her legs shaking, Roz obeyed Sarah.

"We need a different story, now that the damn dog made me bash his head in. Crumpet was running too near the edge of the balcony, and you went after him. The railing is weak, and you both fell."

Roz stopped at the sliding glass door. Sarah had managed to wrestle the gun away from her after it had been fired. The woman's strength was superhuman, fueled by a hatred Roz was only beginning to understand.

"Open the door and get out on that balcony!"

Knowing she was too clever to shoot her and leave contradictory evidence, Roz said slowly, "He wanted to love you, Sarah."

"You shut up! You know *nothing* about what was between me and my father, so don't start making up lies now! Move!"

She walked slowly out onto the balcony. It was an architectural masterpiece, seeming to hang suspended over the canyon on thin stilts. She could see other houses in the distance, but the area was fairly secluded.

"Get to the edge. By the railing," Sarah ordered.

Roz did, walking as slowly as she could, her mind working desperately. Could she fight Sarah off out here? Though she didn't want to give up, she knew the odds were overwhelmingly against her. Sarah was stronger. And much more clever at things like this.

"Put your hands behind your back. That's right; hold your wrist in your hand."

Roz looked below her, all the way down. It was hundreds of feet to the bottom. If she and Crumpet were pushed off the balcony, she wondered if there would be anything left of them.

"Now you look down there, Roz. Wouldn't you rather help me with my plan? The dog's already dead, so what's the difference?"

"No." Her reply was barely a whisper.

"You're not only trash, you're stupid."

"No, Sarah. Someone's going to catch on to you. Maybe not this time but soon. There are people who know you murdered Matthew. Don't you think someone's going to start asking questions when I'm found dead?"

"It won't be that boyfriend of a bodyguard you have. He was killed in that accident."

"No." Her voice trembled slightly.

Sarah laughed. "You're touching, Rosalind. You amuse me. How else do you think I got his jacket? I knew you wouldn't come with me unless I had evidence. I hired the man who hit him, and he knew how to do the job. I've been tired of both of you and your ridiculous antics with that damn dog. Now it's only a matter of time before I have it all."

Roz was silent. She wouldn't have thought there was room for any more pain. But at the thought of never seeing Jamie again, she bent her head slightly, her gaze blurred and unfocused.

Sarah was winning.

Oh, Jamie. She couldn't bear to think of the pain he must have suffered. Jamie, who loved life more than anyone she had ever met. And who possessed the gift of being able to share that love and excitement with others. Was it really only days ago she had been in his arms and contemplating what a miracle it was they had found each other? If she closed her eyes, she could see his face. She realized quietly she wanted that to be the last image in her mind before she died.

Help me, Jamie. I've never been that brave. Help me reach you and Matthew and Crumpet, and maybe then we can all find some peace. She had never really had a family, and the time she had spent with Matthew, Crumpet and Jamie—especially Jamie—had been blessed. At least Sarah could never destroy the happiness they'd had. Or the love.

"Rosalind? I'm going to give you one last chance to come to your senses. Once you have your share of the money, you can have anything you want. I'd rather see you walk out of here alive than have to fall off that balcony."

"What you really mean is, it would be more convenient for you." There was a quiet strength to her voice now that she had accepted what lay ahead.

"Yes or no, Rosalind?"

She shook her head. "No."

"I don't understand you."

She smiled. "I didn't think you would."

The canyon seemed perfectly quiet below her. Roz didn't want to hear anymore. She closed her eyes as she heard Sarah coming toward her. Roz knew she was a coward, but she just didn't have the heart to go on.

"Get down!"

The voice seemed to come at her from a dream. She knew whose it was but couldn't believe it was Jamie's. Still, it was a voice she would obey unquestioningly, and she dropped to the rough redwood deck.

There was the sickening crash of splintering wood, then a scream. She closed her eyes tightly as she felt the balcony tremble. Tears began to run down her face as the scream went on and on.

By the time it ended, she felt Jamie's arm around her.

"Jamie?" She was looking up at him, totally confused, her body shaking. "What are you doing here?" It was all she could think to say.

"Roz. Oh, God, I thought I was too late." He cradled her in his arms, and she felt some of the warmth from his body beginning to penetrate hers.

"What—" She looked over the edge of the balcony, but he cupped the back of her head with his palm and pressed her face against his shirt.

"Don't look."

"Did she—"

"She was going to push you against the railing and break it. She went over when you hit the floor."

He helped her back inside the house. It took a moment for her eyes to adjust, but when they did, she went down on her knees and began to crawl toward the center of the large living room.

Crumpet was still lying on the carpet. If she'd known better, she could have pretended he was asleep. When she reached him, she put her palm against his head, and petted him gently. He was still warm.

The feel of his silky fur was her undoing, and she started to cry, then pressed her face against the bulldog's neck. "Oh, Jamie, he tried to stop Sarah from touching me. He never liked to fight, but he grabbed her by the leg, and she hit him with the candlestick."

"Roz." She felt his arm around her shoulder, offering comfort.

"Matthew was right." She was sobbing so hard she could barely force the words out of her mouth. "Crumpet had nothing but heart. He wasn't a fighter. Kai would have known how to fight, but Crumpet didn't. He would never have done it if it hadn't been for me.'' The last words were a harsh whisper, and she started to sob again.

"He loved you, Roz. You couldn't ask for better than that from a dog."

"Oh, Crumpet, why did you have to do it? You knew I wasn't going to give you to her. I would have thought of something. Why did you have to try?''

She was sobbing so hard, she didn't feel the slight trembling beneath her. But as she took a deep, shuddering breath, she heard a soft snort.

"Crumpet?" She slowly sat up, then put her hand on his head. *"Crumpet?"*

Slowly, ever so slowly, one eye fluttered open. Its expression was dazed. Roz put her other hand next to his jaws and felt the tiniest breath.

He whined then, and she gathered him into her arms.

THE POLICE ARRIVED soon after, but she and Jamie left immediately to take Crumpet to Dr. Ramsey's office.

"He's a tough old nut. It'll take more than a crack on the head with a candlestick to put this boy out of commission."

"You're sure he's all right?"

"Rosalind, these dogs were bred to fight bulls. They have tough heads. Just keep him quiet for a few days and make sure he eats."

"That's never been a problem," Jamie said quietly, petting the dog.

"Messy business with Sarah," Dr. Ramsey remarked. "I thought all along it had to be one of the children, but I would have guessed Elizabeth."

"That's what threw us off," Jamie admitted. "She was the one who seemed to have a clear motive. Sarah was more adept at covering her tracks."

"I don't think she ever would have had enough," Roz said slowly. "Even if she had gotten the money, she would have wanted more." She looked up at Jamie. "It never really was the money. I think that was what she thought she wanted, but it was like—she was trying to fill something empty inside her. She'd always have to have more."

"You're right," Jamie said. "In order for Sarah to create Sarah, she had to destroy her father and everything he loved."

Dr. Ramsey spoke quietly as he patted Crumpet. "There was never any doubt in my mind there was foul play connected with Matthew's death. I'm just relieved the whole thing can be laid to rest."

"You're *sure* he's all right?" Roz asked again, indicating Crumpet.

"Just put him to bed and turn on one of those television programs he likes. But watch that he doesn't see a dog on the screen and get overexcited." At Roz's surprised expression, he smiled. "Matthew told me all about it. He used to laugh about it. You should be proud of yourself, young lady. I know Matthew would be."

"I could never have done any of this if it hadn't been for Jamie. And Crumpet."

The older man looked at Roz, then Jamie. "Matthew Barrett was never a man who left anything to chance. I don't think it was simply coincidence the two of you met." He cleared his throat, then scratched Crumpet's chest. "I think it would have made him very happy."

THAT EVENING they celebrated the New Year. Jamie told Olivia Stewart and her husband, Marvin, what had happened that afternoon, and thanked the older woman profusely for providing the key that had enabled him to solve the case.

"When you said it was always the coolest personalities that boiled underneath, I realized that, of the three children, it *had* to be Sarah. Matt and Elizabeth were too volatile. They wouldn't have had the ability to coolly murder their father."

"I told you, Marvin, that my gossiping wasn't a waste of time! And Jamie even thinks I should write a book."

They tuned in the television set in time to see the silver ball fall in Times Square, and they heard the grandfather clock in the library chime midnight. Champagne corks flew, and toasts were made.

"This is the year I write my best-seller!" Olivia announced, her bugle-beaded sheath glittering in the candlelight. "And, Marvin, I want you to represent me."

Her husband merely shook his head and reached for a glass of champagne.

"We're going to have a baby!" Deena told Roz. "Harold thinks we should start a family right away."

"Mom, that's wonderful."

"And this is the year I hope you—" Deena began.

Roz saw her mother's eyes straying toward Jamie. "Mother, don't say a word." Deena merely smiled and glanced at the silver ring on Roz's finger. Roz clenched her fingers into a fist and walked toward Jamie.

He was standing by the tree, talking with Jesse.

"Can I have a quick word with you?" she asked.

They walked out of the hallway, and Roz came straight to the point. "If I don't get rid of my mother, I'm going to scream."

"That bad?"

"Jamie, I try, but she still irritates me."

"Your wish is my command." He pulled her into his arms and lowered his head until their mouths were almost touching. "I see you didn't pay any attention to where I hung the mistletoe."

She smiled up at him, feeling her body start to relax.

"You think you're pretty clever, don't you?"

He kissed her then with a thoroughness that left her weak and pliant, then walked her back into the library.

"If you think I'm clever now, wait until you see how quickly I show the last guest to the door. They'll never know what hit them."

He was as good as his word.

When the last guest left, Jamie and Roz left the mess downstairs and retreated to the bedroom. He had saved one last bottle of champagne, and Roz took it upstairs with them. Jamie was busily carrying Crumpet.

"I could really build up my muscles hefting this guy around," he said. The bulldog swiped at his cheek with his tongue.

Once settled on the bed, Roz picked up the remote control and turned on the set.

"What'll it be tonight, Crumpet? There's a musical on Channel Nine, a rock video program on Forty. There's a western on Thirteen—"

She began flicking channels, then stopped as Crumpet gave a short, sharp bark. That was his signal that he liked what was on the television.

"What is this?" A black Ferrari was squealing around the corner, a rock-and-roll song throbbing in the background.

"C'mon, Roz, you've watched enough television in the last few months. You should know."

"I've never seen this show before."

Two men jumped out of the Ferrari and ran into a pale pink stucco building. Crumpet was lying on the very edge of the bed, his front paws hanging over the side, his eyes glued to the set.

The dialogue was short, staccato. "Freeze! Miami Vice!"

"Wait a minute," Roz began.

"Peach, everyone needs a fantasy, even bulldogs."

"Crumpet, don't you go getting any ideas."

At the mention of his name, Crumpet barked. His stubby tail was wriggling, his back paws dug into the bedclothes. When the sound of stereo gunshots filled the bedroom, he barked again and cocked his head.

"Think about it, Peach. I'd be the only private investigator who'd have his own bulldog. Sort of like Mike Hammer meets Jaws."

"Don't even joke about it. I've had enough adventure to last me a lifetime."

As Crumpet settled down to watch drug smuggling in Miami, Jamie popped open the last bottle of champagne and poured two glasses.

"To the new year, Roz."

"It can't be any worse than the old."

"Oh, I don't know about you, but I kind of liked this year."

"I liked parts of it."

"Which parts?"

"Don't fish."

"Tell me." He reached for the bottle of champagne and refilled her glass. "Or I'll get you so soused you'll be spilling state secrets all over the place."

"Anything but that!" She took another sip of champagne and lay back in bed. "The best part was you. How's that?"

"Go on." His expression was intent.

She decided the time was right to reveal how she felt about their relationship. "I've never been as close to anyone as you, Jamie. I don't know how you did it, but you got past all the defenses I normally set up."

"Clever investigating," he said softly, but his eyes were serious.

"It's been better than any movie I've ever watched."

He eased her into his arms, and she looked up into his eyes, seeing everything she had ever wanted to see in his expression. He loved her. And she knew, with a deep certainty, he would never leave her.

"If we got through all this today, don't you think it kind of means we're meant to do something?" she asked.

He nodded. "I know what you mean. But right now I have more immediate plans in mind."

"Such as—"

"Such as finishing that bottle of champagne and having my wicked way with you. All to the tune of a Busby Berkeley musical."

She laughed then as his lips came down over hers.

THREE GLASSES OF CHAMPAGNE apiece and a few hours later, they were stretched out in bed in each other's arms.

"The only good thing I can say about today," Roz said slowly, "is that it really taught me what's important."

"And what's that?"

"You and me and Crumpet."

"So you really would be upset if I bought Crumpet a shoulder holster."

"Jamie, don't joke. This is serious. I don't think— I'm not sure I can live with the fact that you might not come home at night."

"Roz, ninety-nine percent of a private investigator's work isn't half as dangerous as this was. Most of it's pretty simple stuff, missing persons and all that."

"Are you sure?"

"Positive."

She traced a line on his chest with her forefinger, frowning. "If a case that fell into that one percent turned up, would you give it to someone else?"

"Is it that important to you?" He was serious now.

"Yeah." Her eyes filled with tears. "I couldn't go through today again. When I was standing out on the balcony and Sarah told me you'd been killed—"

"She told you that?" She felt his body tense, and he levered himself up, then said softly, "She was a sick woman, Roz. The whole thing was sick."

"I can't live with it, Jamie."

"I won't ask you to." He stretched out full-length on the bed, then patted his chest. "C'mere."

She went back into his arms and turned her head so she could see his face.

"I was thinking, is there anything in the will that prevents you from putting some of Matthew's money to work right now?"

"I don't know. I guess I could as long as Crumpet is properly taken care of."

"I think that would be pretty exciting work."

"The Matthew Barrett Foundation," she breathed softly. "Or maybe just the Barrett Foundation. Oh, Jamie, he would have loved it!"

He smiled down at her. "I don't think I'll miss investigating that much. I was beginning to burn out, and this case just about finished me off."

"It would be so exciting, putting together something like that."

"Nothing's quite as exciting as seeing dreams come true. And anyway," he said, tracing her cheekbone with his finger, "I have this funny feeling we're going to keep things exciting around here for a long, long time."

EARLY NEW YEAR'S DAY she felt Jamie nudging her gently.

"Hmm?"

"Look over by the television."

She had left it on, and Crumpet was curled up on a cushion, watching his favorite Busby Berkeley tape. She'd turned the sound down low, and Mickey Rooney and Judy Garland were marching in front of a band.

The slight movement on Crumpet's side caught her eye. Rocky was watching the screen intently, her head resting on Crumpet's pillow. The setter leaned over and gave Crumpet a quick swipe with her tongue.

"I knew she'd come out someday." She lay back in bed and sighed, content. "That's about the best start to a new year I can think of."

"I can think of a better one."

"I bet you can."

He surprised her then, rolling away from her and reaching into the drawer of the nightstand. When he handed her the small jeweler's box, she stared at him.

"I was going to give you this big line about how we couldn't split up because it would break Crumpet's heart. And then I thought I should give you more time. But after what we went through, I decided I didn't want to wait anymore."

The ring was stunning, a diamond in a platinum setting.

"I don't know what to say. Jamie—"

"Just say yes. The rest will be easy."

"Yes."

After he kissed her, he said, "We could drive to Vegas. It's the only place I can think of that'll have a chapel open on New Year's Day." He hesitated for a moment. "Unless you want a big wedding."

"Not unless you do."

The mattress quivered, and she glanced to the foot of the bed. The tape had come to a commercial, and Crumpet had jumped up on the bed. He walked up the bedclothes until he was practically on top of Jamie's chest, then gave him a quick slurp on his cheek.

"Don't tell me Vegas is in his vocabulary."

"It wouldn't be a honeymoon without Crumpet. I've kind of gotten used to the three of us together."

He scratched the back of the bulldog's head, and Crumpet snorted contentedly. "We'll take him along. I wouldn't want to leave him alone so soon after that whack on the head."

Soft music swelled from the television, and Crumpet cocked his ears in the direction it was coming from. Another musical was starting. He clumsily turned around and trotted to the edge of the bed, then jumped down onto the floor.

"He comes along on one condition," Jamie said, grasping her hip with his fingers and pulling her close.

"Separate suites?"

"And his has to have a wide-screen television and VCR."

She kissed his cheek. "I won't let you forget the tapes."

Epilogue

The phone rang, and Rosalind leaned forward in her desk chair and picked up the receiver.

"Barrett Foundation. May I help you?" She listened to the woman's impassioned voice, then smiled as she recognized the symptoms.

"No, your cat hasn't broken her back legs. She's in heat. You said she was around six months old? Then she's right on schedule."

The woman asked her several other questions, which Roz answered to the best of her ability.

"I'd keep her inside. We strongly urge pet owners to spay and neuter their animals, as the pet population in this country has become overwhelming. We have a free spaying clinic every Friday afternoon. If you don't have a way to get here, we can send one of our vans to pick up you and your cat. But please think it over, Mrs. Corsino. If you took one walk through our shelter and saw how many kittens and cats we have, I'm sure you'd agree with me." She talked with the woman for several more minutes, then hung up the phone and stretched her legs underneath the desk.

Somehow it had all worked out. When she and Jamie had decided to make Matthew's dreams become reality, they had had no idea of the amount of work involved. But somehow, over the last three years, they had done it. The Barrett Foundation was one of the largest animal welfare organizations in the country, with offices across the United States. They were opening their first overseas office next spring in London and then branching out around the globe. Matthew would have been proud of the foundation. And he would have been so pleased that his grandson, Mark, now eleven, worked some Saturdays at the Los Angeles branch.

Roz studied the picture of Crumpet and Matthew on her desk, then turned her head to see the former fast asleep in the bay window of her office. She and Jamie and several of their dogs had driven up from Los Angeles for two weeks of work in the San Francisco office. It was an old Victorian house overlooking the Bay. They had bought the houses on either side and fenced in the entire area, so there was plenty of room for the foundation to continue to grow.

Crumpet yawned, and she studied him. The bulldog was eight years old now and slowing down. There were a few white hairs around his dark muzzle, and he wasn't as quick as he'd been as a pup—except where food was concerned. Curled up next to Crumpet was the love of his life, a fawn-colored female bulldog named Petunia. Jamie's mother had brought Petunia down with her when she'd come to visit her son after his whirlwind marriage in Las Vegas. Roz had been terribly scared about not measuring up to some invisible standard, but the moment she had opened the door and seen the tall woman with twinkling eyes dressed in her tweed suit and sensible shoes, she had liked Jamie's mother. Meryl was a one-of-a-kind character. Brisk and no-nonsense, she had stepped inside the mansion and handed Roz Petunia's leash.

"It's time Crumpet had more on his mind than his next meal," she'd said. And Roz had agreed.

Crumpet had come thundering down the hall as soon as he heard the bell. When he first saw Petunia standing next to Roz, he'd stood perfectly still, his ears cocked forward, his nostrils quivering. Then he had yapped once, then twice, then turned around and sped down the hall. Roz had knelt down and unsnapped Petunia's leash, and the female bulldog had raced off after Crumpet.

"One thing I'll say for Petunia, she isn't shy," Meryl had said briskly. "You must be Rosalind. I'm delighted to finally meet you. Matthew spoke so highly of you. And Jamie—well, I'm glad he came to his senses and decided to keep you in the family."

At that moment, Roz had fallen in love. Years later, she realized she finally had the family she had always yearned for. Eventually, she met all of Jamie's family, and they welcomed her, making her feel she had always been a part of their happiness and warmth.

It was Crumpet who had really gone on to become something of a celebrity. After the horrifying afternoon spent at Sarah's house, word had leaked out that the "Billion-Dollar Baby" had defended his mistress against all odds and almost gotten himself killed in the process. Roz and Jamie had been deluged with offers. America was ready for a hero again, and Crumpet filled the bill to perfection.

Roz had chosen his projects carefully. She agreed to do an interview with Barbara Walters and tell the truth about what had happened, simply because she wanted to squelch the rumors and half-truths. When she'd come to the part of her story where she'd thought Crumpet was dead, there wasn't a dry eye among the cast and crew. She also agreed to do several magazine articles, and Crumpet's picture graced the covers of *Good Housekeeping, Esquire, Newsweek, Time* and *Dog World*.

She and Jamie decided to use Crumpet's newfound fame to launch the Barrett Foundation and a public-awareness campaign concerning animals. The "Have a Heart" campaign was their most successful, and Crumpet's television spots brought the reality of needy and abused animals home to the American public. They were swamped with mail. Grade-school class-rooms across the country sent them their nickels and dimes; teenagers offered to volunteer in their neigh-borhoods to pick up strays. Money and support came in from the most unlikely sources, and even though Matthew's fortune took care of the brunt of the foun-dation's financial needs, it was gratifying to know the American public was rallying.

There was time for fun, as well. Roz let Crumpet appear on one of his favorite prime-time soaps, and the bulldog stole the show the week he was on, play-ing the part of an oil baron's pet. He also appeared on an ABC after-school special that dealt with abuse of domestic animals. A TV movie-of-the-week was made of his life, and though Crumpet did not play himself, both he and Roz were present on the set to ensure the script achieved authenticity. The screenwriter handled the subject with taste and restraint, and the movie swept the ratings the week it was on. He even had a breakfast cereal, "Crumpet's Crunchies," named after him, with all profits going to the foundation.

But the highlight of Crumpet's television career was a spot he shared with the First Lady concerning drug abuse. The dialogue was crisp and to the point. "Crumpet and I both agree—when you're approached by a stranger who offers you drugs, you should just say no. Isn't that right, Crumpet?" And Crumpet had barked sharply, then looked straight into Camera Three to give the public his by-then famous snort.

When Crumpet finally saw himself on television, he was stunned. Roz and Jamie taped all of his television appearances, and Crumpet found them fascinating. He and Rocky watched them for hours. Petunia never learned to like television, so Crumpet had to learn the art of compromise and spend a good part of his day playing in the backyard.

Roz started as she felt something nudge her hand. Brought back to the present, she glanced down at her desk and saw that the tiny gray-and-white kitten that had been asleep on a stack of her paperwork was ready to play. It batted at her hand with its tiny paw, and she petted the downy head with one of her fingers. The kitten had been brought in yesterday morning by a little boy who had found him in a garbage can. It was so small, Roz had taken on this project herself.

Reaching into her desk drawer, she found a can of soft food and popped the lid open. The kitten was old enough to eat solid food but so thin it looked younger. Sliding the can across the desk until it was underneath the kitten's nose, she stroked its back gently as it began to eat.

There had been other changes in the past three years. Perhaps the most significant was the way she felt about herself. Roz had always believed something was lacking in her, whether it was a formal education or a solid family background. Yet as she and Jamie continued to build the Barrett Foundation, both of them had been called upon to use talents they'd never imagined they'd possessed. They had both grown with the shelter, and looking back, Roz realized she had finally come to accept her past and make peace with herself.

There were things she could do, things she was good at. She could reach people on an emotional level. She could encourage the most ornery individual to accept the obligation he had to other forms of life on Earth besides his own. She could talk to a crowd of people in a shopping mall or church hall or a YMCA and help them understand that everyone had a responsibility and in the end it came down to individual actions making the world a better place. And she could work. Long after other volunteers had gone home, she and Jamie would still be filing, answering phones, figuring out new ways to reach the public and educate them.

It was a never-ending process, but one she loved intensely. And as she learned to do new things and accept new challenges, Roz learned to like herself.

A lot of that had to do with Jamie, too. She picked up another framed picture and studied the photo of herself, Jamie and Crumpet in front of the twenty-four-hour chapel in Las Vegas. She was dressed in the glittering silver dress, Jamie in a tuxedo. Crumpet had a bow around his neck. It had been a crazy wedding. The minister—also an Elvis impersonator—had let Crumpet be a witness. Their marriage license had a chubby dog print on the side. And then, after he'd married them, the minister had said, "Just take that piece of paper and tuck it away somewhere. Don't start thinking of yourselves as married. Just love each other, treat each other kindly, and it will all work out."

They had thanked him, then checked into one of Vegas's more garish hotels.

But you almost didn't get there at all, she thought, then leaned back in her chair and grinned.

They had started driving New Year's Day after quickly packing and making sure Jesse was available to take care of the animals, especially Rocky. Once on the road, they had both felt like children the night before Christmas. She hadn't questioned the suddenness of their decision, because it had simply felt so *right*. She had allowed Jamie to come closer then anyone else because she trusted and loved him. Any problems could be worked out with time.

An hour and a half out of Los Angeles, they'd pulled into a McDonald's. Leaving Crumpet briefly in the car—parked where they could see him—they had gone inside and ordered. Once they were back in the car, they realized they wouldn't be going anywhere for a short period of time.

Crumpet had fallen asleep on the gas pedal, flooding the car.

"I think," said Roz as she reached for a french fry, "that perhaps it's his way of telling us to consider this marriage carefully. Perhaps we shouldn't rush into this.''

''What do you mean?'' There had been a glint of uneasiness in his eyes, and Roz couldn't seriously keep him in suspense.

''It's just that—I can't marry a man when I don't know what his initials stand for.''

He smiled, then popped another Chicken Mc-Nugget into Crumpet's waiting mouth. ''You couldn't just accept the fact that I'm a man of mystery?''

''Is it your first name or your middle name?''

''First. James is my middle name.''

''So you've never been called by your real first name?''

''Not since I had any say in the matter.''

''I could take a peek at your birth certificate.''

''But you won't. I know you, Roz.''

''Is it something really horrible, Jamie? I mean, like Thurston or Thornbill?''

''Worse.''

''In what way?''

''It's a wimpy name.''

''Wimpy?''

He leaned back in the driver's seat, his arm along the top of the seat as he played with a strand of her hair. ''I'm going to give you one enormous clue; then I don't want to talk about this anymore.''

''It'd better be enormous, then.''

''It will be, Peach.'' He took a deep breath. ''Your mother wasn't the only one who read historical romances when she was pregnant.''

There was a short silence; then Roz said softly, ''Trenton?''

"Close."

She closed her eyes and thought furiously for several seconds. The name floated into her mind, and she blurted it out.

"Tristan."

He closed his eyes and nodded his head wearily.

"Tristan? Really?"

"As in Tristan and Isolde."

"Oh, my God."

"You see what I mean."

"Yeah."

Crumpet snorted from the back seat, and Roz automatically gave him another McNugget.

"Just about everyone in the world knows me as James or Jamie or even Jim. I just never felt the name was . . . *me*."

"Did you ever get teased about it in school?" she asked softly.

"Every year. You know how teachers read the roll call the first day at school? Each year I came home with a bloody nose because some jerk would make a crack about my name and I'd have to defend myself."

"Did the other guy look just as bad?"

He smiled slowly. "Well, yeah. But I've never enjoyed fighting."

"When did you change your name?"

"In the seventh grade. I've been Jamie ever since."

She put her hand on his arm. "Your secret will follow me to my grave."

"I'd appreciate it."

"I won't even consider naming any of my animals Tristan."

"That would be a blessing."

"And if we ever have any children—"

"They'll have nice, normal names and never have to worry about bloody noses or children laughing at them or having to use their middles names or initials."

"That about covers it."

Once they were able to start the car, they covered the distance to Vegas quickly and found the chapel. It was garish, with neon wedding bells above the entrance and flashing letters, but Roz fell in love with it at first sight.

"It's us, Jamie."

"Definitely."

But before they had walked in the front door, he'd stopped her.

"There's something else you have to know about me, Roz."

"More names?"

"No, nothing like that. It's just..." He looked down at the cement for a moment.

"Jamie, you can tell me. Nothing's going to stop me from feeling the way I do about you."

"This could be difficult." He took a deep breath. "Okay, Peach, I swore to myself I would never deceive you. And I never intended to, but after what we went through, I just wanted us to get married and be together for the rest of our lives. But there are some pretty crucial things we haven't really discussed that I think people who are considering getting married need to talk about."

"You don't want children. Even with normal names."

"No, I still want a family. I want some years alone with you first, but that hasn't changed."

"You've never really cared for Crumpet." Now she was getting uneasy.

"No, no, I love all the animals."

Comprehension dawned. "It's the money. Oh, Jamie, I don't think of it as mine or even Crumpet's. Matthew left it to us as a *tool*, as a way of making a difference. But it isn't mine. I'd love you if you were a pauper. I don't think about stuff like that."

He had turned pale, and she touched his arm, then guided him over to a wrought-iron bench outside the chapel entrance. Winged cupids and bows were woven into the ironwork, and the flashing neon was almost above them, adding a surrealistic quality to their surroundings.

Jamie sat down heavily, then turned toward her and took both her hands in his. "I haven't been completely honest with you, Roz."

She felt her throat go dry. "Are you—is there someone—I mean, are you already married or something?"

"No, it's just—the entire time we lived at Matthew's, you talked about how much you disliked money and what it did to people. And I know you saw all this going on among Matthew's family and the way they treated each other, but—Roz, it doesn't have to be that way."

She felt as if she were slowly brushing away cobwebs and trying to see something clearly. "Are you trying to tell me—Jamie, do you—are you—"

He nodded.

"I mean, are we talking about an enormous amount of—"

He nodded again.

"Filthy rich?"

Not looking at her, he nodded his head a final time.

There was a short silence; then Roz squeezed his hand. "We can work it out, Jamie. It's not like I think something like that would ever come between us."

"I just didn't know what you'd think."

She cleared her throat. "Do you want me to sign one of those agreements?"

"No, this is for keeps, Roz. I think we both know that."

She let go of his hands and stood up, then walked slightly away from the bench in the direction of their parked car. Crumpet trotted behind her. She folded her arms in front of her and gazed out into the neon night sky.

She felt Jamie come up behind her, but he didn't touch her. Another couple walked by them, obviously on their way to the chapel. Once they were inside and out of hearing, Roz spoke.

"I guess the only way I feel is just a little stupid. Here all I did while we lived together at the mansion was talk about how much I hated living there and what the money was doing to everyone. You must have thought I was pretty ignorant."

"I thought you were right."

She chose her words carefully. "Then it can be different." She felt his hands close over her shoulders, could feel the warmth of his touch through the sparkling silver material. He had insisted she wear the silver gown she'd first worn when they danced on the terrace. He turned her toward him, then put a finger underneath her chin and raised her face to his.

"Yes, it can." He took a deep breath. "My mother isn't like Katherine. *You* aren't like Katherine. Money isn't the only thing you live for. It makes a difference when you can keep it in persepctive."

They were both silent for a moment; then he said softly, "Something's still bugging you; I can tell."

She concentrated on his chin, not daring to meet his eyes. When she spoke, her voice was low. "It's just that I feel—I mean, I'm not bringing much to this marriage, then. You know everything about me, Jamie. About my life and what I've done and what I *haven't* done. I hope I can fit into your world."

"You already do." He gave her a quick, hard hug, then stepped back and tucked her arm into his. "Come on; let's go."

"Are you sure?"

He touched her cheek gently. "Peach, there are a lot of different ways to feel rich. And right now I feel like one of the richest people in the world. I get to marry you."

She could feel her eyes filling, and she blinked rapidly.

"No crying, now. Brides only get to cry *during* the ceremony."

"Okay." She sniffed, then smiled. "Okay, I can do it now."

And though her voice quavered as she recited her vows, the next time she kissed Jamie, she was his wife. And she promised herself she would spend the rest of her life making sure he never regretted marrying her.

Roz was eased back to the present when she felt a rough little tongue licking her thumb. The kitten had finished almost half the can and was washing itself, giving her a few swipes in between. Smiling, she picked up the tiny animal and cradled it in her arms.

The phone buzzed again, and she picked it up.

"Your husband is on his way up, Rosalind."

"Thanks, Maura." She hung up the phone and got up from behind her desk. She was halfway to the door when it opened and Jamie walked in, Rocky on her leash behind him.

"It all worked out," he said, catching her and the kitten in a quick hug, then giving her a kiss.

"He can keep his dog?" Jamie had been out on a call, visiting an older man whose children wanted him to enter a nursing home. But none of them wanted to take in the dog, and none of the homes in the Bay area accepted animals along with the residents.

"He agreed that if we could keep the animal at our special shelter and he could visit him whenever he wanted, he would give the home a try."

"And maybe we can work something else out later."

"There's got to be a better solution." He glanced at Crumpet and Petunia, curled up together in the sun. "Is everybody ready to go?"

"Just about. Do you think your sister would want another cat?" she asked, petting the kitten, which now had its tiny claws firmly embedded in her sweatshirt.

"I think you can talk her into it. Mom's expecting us for dinner. She made a roast, so we'd better—"

The phone buzzed again, and Roz shot her husband a questioning look.

"Take it. But then we'd better get going."

As she walked back over to her desk, Jamie went over to Crumpet and petted him on the head. The bulldog raised his head, blinking sleepily.

"Roast, Crumpet."

He stood up and stretched, then jumped down and sat at Jamie's feet.

Roz picked up the receiver and punched the blinking button. "You've reached the Barrett Foundation. Can I help— What? Oh, no. You're sure about that?"

Jamie scratched Crumpet's ears. "I have this horrible feeling, old buddy, that we're not going to make it home in time for dinner."

"How much money did you say is involved?" Roz asked, then reached for a pad and pen. "And you're sure about that? Yes, we can help you. We have our own special group of lawyers who are involved with animal rights. Yes, I can understand how you'd be scared. Tonight?"

"Like I said, Crumpet, forget the roast," Jamie said.

Crumpet slowly lay down, put his head between his paws and whined.

"I'll be over as soon as I can, I promise you. Now let me read your address back—"

"Here we go again."

When Roz hung up, she grabbed her knapsack and down jacket. "Jamie, this woman called, and it seems her grandmother died a few days ago. The will was read, and she left her entire fortune to her three Siamese cats, and her children—"

"Whoa, Roz, let's take it one step at a time. Do we have to go over there now?"

"I think so. She said it was really ugly. They threatened her and everything because her grandmother left her in charge—"

"Who said? Roz, slow down."

"Her granddaughter. She was left in charge as executrix of the estate. Her grandmother had a mansion up in Marin County, but no one really had any idea how much money she had tucked away until they found out what she was leaving the cats."

"And so her children are threatening the granddaughter."

"Exactly. I want to move them out of the house for now and have police protection arranged. She said they already tried to kill one of the cats, and she's scared to stay in the mansion alone."

"Why don't I call my mother and tell her we'll be having four more to dinner?"

"Could we do that? I just hate to leave her alone."

"I think I've heard this song before. Don't worry, Roz, we can handle it."

THAT NIGHT, curled up in Jamie's bed in his old room at his mother's house, Roz watched her husband as he stood in the bathroom and brushed his teeth. Their new friend and her three Siamese cats were settled in the guest bedroom down the hall.

When Jamie clicked off the bathroom light and came over to the bed, she slid over and put her arms around him as he settled in beside her.

"I feel so awful for her, Jamie. It brought so many of those old feelings back. Remember?"

"Uh-huh." He gave her shoulder a quick squeeze, then moved slightly so he was looking down at her upturned face.

"But you do remember our deal, don't you?"

The deal had been struck in the early days of creating the Barrett Foundation. As the work was so all-consuming, she and Jamie had reached an agreement that all shoptalk ceased when they reached their bedroom. Then their time was for each other.

"Yeah, I do. I'm sorry."

"Don't be. I know you're concerned."

"Can I have just three minutes, Jamie, and then I promise nothing more for the rest of the night."

"Okay."

"I was thinking a lot about Matthew today, and I was remembering so much of what we talked about. He used to tell me he believed one person could make a difference. And as much as I was upset for that girl today, I was glad she had someone to turn to. And I thought that if everything hadn't happened the way it had, I never would have met you, and none of this would have happened."

Jamie lay back on his side, then traced her cheekbone with his forefinger.

"Peach, he would have gotten us together sooner or later. It was only a matter of time."

"You think so?"

"I know so." He glanced at a mock watch on his wrist. "Now, your three minutes are up, and I think it's time we gave some serious thought as to tonight's agenda."

"Why, whatever do you mean?" But she ran her fingers lightly over his arm, then pressed her palm against the warmth of his chest.

"Hey, I can't help it if you find me irresistible."

She moved her hand lower, touching him playfully.

He sucked in his breath sharply. "And of course the feeling is mutual." His voice was strained.

"I like to think so."

He kissed her for a long time, then eased her up over him until they were as close as two people can be.

"You're right about one thing, Peach," he whispered softly, and she felt herself melting at the sound of his voice.

"What's that?"

"One person can make all the difference in the world."

"Yeah?" She kissed him, loving the feel of her bare breasts against his chest. "Then show me."

Harlequin American Romance

COMING NEXT MONTH

#165 LE CLUB by Beverly Sommers

Wynn Ransome was Le Club's most eligible male, high praise considering the clientele of the chic Manhattan health spot. Terry Caputo was there to catch a murderer. They met on the exercise bikes, and Wynn made his first move. As duty warred with destiny, Terry feared her stakeout was about to become a date.

#166 THE DEVLIN DARE by Cathy Gillen Thacker

Marine boot camp did strange things to people. Mollie Devlin thought she'd taken leave of her senses. When her bunk buddy dared her to make a conquest of dynamic Dave Talmadge, Mollie set out to win Dave's heart. Unfortunately, she never stopped to consider the dangerous consequences.

#167 AFTER THE STORM by Rebecca Flanders

Every time Kevin breezed into his hometown, he demolished Kate's groceries and ran up her phone bill, proving that TV's ultimate sex symbol was actually the ultimate nuisance. Until one night when the wind began to roar through Victoria Bend, Mississippi, and there was only Kevin to teach Kate a lesson in heroism and once-in-a-lifetime love.

#168 OPPOSITES ATTRACT by Karen Pershing

Could opposites attract? The answer was no. But could opposites get along? For Carrie the answer was the same. She simply didn't want to get involved with a man who wore impeccable three-piece suits. But no matter how hard Carrie tried to convince herself of that, Max tried even harder to create the impossible.

WIN GREAT PRIZES
Claim Lots of Free Gifts

If you missed our ad in the center section of this novel, use the coupon below.

We'll send you lots of free gifts just for trying our Reader Service…4 full-length current stories of love and romance, an elegant velveteen jewelry bag, and a surprise free gift, one that will really delight you.

FREE gifts!

AND we'll also automatically qualify you for all featured prizes in our Super Celebration Sweepstakes…prizes like A Dozen Roses + a Dozen Crisp $100 bills—birthstone earrings—your choice of a stunning Mink or Fox Jacket—mounds of delicious Godiva Chocolates—an Island-in-the-Sun vacation for 2—and Perfume Collections direct from France.

FREE prizes!

There is no catch, no obligation when you say YES to all this. We'll simply send you collections of our newest and best love stories every month or so…AND YOU DECIDE. Keep what you like at big discounts off store prices, with free home delivery in the bargain. Return all others postpaid. Even quit the Service anytime, no questions asked.

BIG SAVINGS!

All gifts and prizes you win are yours no matter what. Simply fill in Coupon below, clip and mail—TODAY!

MAIL TO *Harlequin Reader Service*

IN U.S.A.: 901 Fuhrmann Blvd. Box #1867, Buffalo NY 14240
IN CANADA: Box #2800, 5170 Yonge St. Postal Station A Willowdale, Ontario M2N 6J3

YES, I'll try the Harlequin Reader Service under the terms specified above. Send me 4 FREE BOOKS and all other FREE GIFTS. I understand that I also automatically qualify for ALL Super Celebration prizes and prize features advertised in 1986.

NAME _____

ADDRESS _____ APT # _____

CITY _____ STATE/PROV. _____ ZIP/POST CODE _____

> **BIRTHDAY INFORMATION**
>
> MONTH _____
>
> DAY _____
> We'll tell you on your birthday what you win.

Gift offer limited to new subscribers, 1 per household & terms & prices subject to change. No purchase necessary. Check this box ☐ if you only want to enter Sweeps for single set of prizes—fur jacket and candies.

SWT

Harlequin "Super Celebration"
SWEEPSTAKES

NEW PRIZES—NEW PRIZE FEATURES & CHOICES—MONTHLY

1. To enter the sweepstakes, follow the instructions outlined on the Center Insert Card. Alternate means of entry, NO PURCHASE NECESSARY, you may also enter by mailing your name, address and birthday on a plain 3" x 5" piece of paper to: In U.S.A.: Harlequin "Super Celebration" Sweepstakes, P.O. Box 1867, Buffalo, N.Y. 14240-1867. In Canada: Harlequin "Super Celebration" Sweepstakes, P.O. Box 2800, 5170 Yonge Street, Postal Station A, Willowdale, Ontario M2N 6J3.

2. Winners will be selected in random drawings from all entries received. All prizes will be awarded. These prizes are in addition to any free gifts which might be offered. Versions of this sweepstakes with different prizes may appear in other presentations by TorStar and their affiliates. The maximum value of the prizes offered is $6,000.00. Winners selected will receive the prize offered from their prize package.

3. The selection of winners will be conducted under the supervision of Marden-Kane, an independent judging organization. By entering the sweepstakes, each entrant accepts and agrees to be bound by these rules and the decision of the judges which shall be final and binding. Odds of winning are dependent upon the total number of entries received. Taxes, if any, are the sole responsibility of the winners. Prizes are not transferable. This sweepstakes is scheduled to appear in Retail Outlets of Harlequin Books during the period of June 1986 to December 1986. All entries must be received by January 31st, 1987. The drawing will take place on or about March 1st, 1987 at the offices of Marden-Kane, Lake Success, New York. For Quebec (Canada) residents, any litigation regarding the running of this sweepstakes and the awarding of prizes must be submitted to La Regie de Lotteries et Course du Quebec.

4. This presentation offers the prizes as illustrated on the Center Insert Card.

5. This offer is open to residents of the U.S., and Canada, 18 years or older, except employees of TorStar, its affilliates, subsidiaries, Marden-Kane and all other agencies and persons connected with conducting this sweepstakes. All Federal, State and local laws apply. Void where prohibited or restricted by law. Winners will be notified by mail and may be required to execute an affidavit of eligibility and release which must be returned within 14 days after notification. Winners consent to the use of their name, photograph and/or likeness for advertising and publicity in conjunction with this and similar promotions without additional compensation. One prize per family or household. Canadian winners will be required to answer a skill testing question.

6. For a list of our most recent prize winners, send a stamped, self-addressed envelope to: WINNERS LIST, c/o Marden-Kane, P.O. Box 525, Sayreville, NJ 08872.

*No Lucky Number
needed to win!*

Explore love with Harlequin in the Middle Ages, the Renaissance, in the Regency, the Victorian and other eras.

Relive within these books the endless ages of romance, set against authentic historical backgrounds. Two new historical love stories published each month.